THE DEVELOPMENT OF THOUGHT

Jean Piaget THE
DEVELOPMENT
OF THOUGHT

Equilibration of
Cognitive Structures

TRANSLATED BY ARNOLD ROSIN

THE VIKING PRESS *New York*

L'Equilibration des structures cognitives

© 1975, Presses Universitaires de France

English language translation Copyright
© Viking Penguin Inc., 1977

First published in 1977 by The Viking Press
625 Madison Avenue, New York, N.Y. 10022

Published simultaneously in Canada by
Penguin Books Canada Limited

LIBRARY OF CONGRESS CATALOGING IN PUBLICATION DATA
Piaget, Jean, 1896–
The development of thought.
Translation of L'équilibration
des structures cognitives.
Includes index.
1. Cognition (Child psychology) I. Title.
BF723.C5P49313   155.4'13   76-51308
ISBN 0-670-27070-9

Printed in the United States of America
Set in Linotype Janson

Preface

This work constitutes a complete recast of volume II of *Etudes d'épistémologie génétique* entitled *Logique et équilibre*. The models then used clearly proved to be insufficient, and it was important therefore to restudy the problem completely, particularly as this area of investigation dominates every question on the development of knowledge. The central idea is that knowledge proceeds neither solely from the experience of objects nor from an innate programming performed in the subject but from successive constructions, the result of the constant development of new structures. With this hypothesis, we can refer only to those methods required for regulations leading not to static forms of equilibrium but to reequilibrations which improve the previous structures. That is why we will be speaking of equilibration as a process—and not only of equilibriums—and above all of "increasing equilibrations" as the manner of correcting and completing the preceding forms of equilibriums.

This new volume of *Etudes*, like the preceding one, is the result of the activities of the International Center of Genetic

Epistemology and was made possible by the continuous support of the Swiss National Fund for Scientific Research and The Ford Foundation to which we express our deepest thanks.

Contents

II: *The Construction of Structures*

III: *General Questions*

I

The Process
of Equilibration

One

POSITION OF THE
PROBLEMS AND
EXPLANATORY PROPOSITIONS

This is an attempt to explain the development, perhaps even the formation of knowledge by considering a central process of equilibration. By this we do not mean we can identify a single general structure of equilibrium which can be stated once and for all, and applied to every situation and to every level as Gestalt theorists (inspired by the "field" laws) use their hypothesis for the psychology of form, but rather we can observe a process (hence the term "equilibration") leading from certain states of equilibrium to others, qualitatively different, and passing through multiple "nonbalances" and reequilibrations. Thus the problems to be solved involve various forms of equilibrium, the reasons for nonbalance, and above all the causal mechanisms, or methods, of equilibrations and reequilibrations. It is especially important to stress from the very beginning the fact that, in certain cases, the reequilibrations merely form returns to previous equilibriums; however, those that are fundamental

3

for development consist, on the contrary, in the formations not only of new equilibriums but also in general of better equilibriums. We can, therefore, speak of "increasing equilibrations," and raise the question of self-organization. This first chapter will be devoted to our propositions concerning these processes.

§ *1* /　*The Equilibrium of Cognitive Systems*

With the exception of the balances achieved in actual work, the cognitive equilibriums are quite different from mechanical equilibriums which conserve themselves without modifications or, in the case of "displacement," give rise merely to "moderations" of the disturbance and not to whole compensations. They differ even more from thermodynamic equilibrium (except when it is reversible), which is a state of rest after destruction of structures. On the other hand, cognitive equilibriums are closer to those stationary but dynamic states, mentioned by Prigogine,[1] with exchanges capable of "building and maintaining a functional and structural order in an open system," and they resemble above all the static, biological equilibriums (homeostasis) or dynamic equilibriums ("homeorhesis").

Like the organisms, the cognitive systems are actually both open in the sense that they undergo exchanges with the milieu and closed insofar as they undergo "cycles." Let us call A, B, C, etc., the parts forming such a cycle and A', B', C', etc., the elements of the milieu required to feed the system. We can then formulate a structure whose diagram is:[2]

$$(A \times A') \to B, (B \times B') \to C, \ldots, (Z \times Z') \to (A \times A'),$$

etc.

---

[1] Glansdorf and Prigogine, *Structure, stabilité et fluctuations*, Paris, Masson, 1971, p. 271.

[2] With naturally the possibility of varied short circuits or intersections, etc.

Moreover, it is worth adding a differentiation of the total system to the hierarchized subsystems with similar structures which are linked by connections that are also cyclic.[3] We then see the origin of such forms of equilibrium, since they are the result of the conservation actions which the elements or the subsystems exert upon one another; the forces oppose each other to produce a balance in a mechanical equilibrium. (Let us note that in a logical system the negations are implied, i.e., the forces are mutually conserved.) Such a conservation action is readily applied to a total system by the subsystems or their elements and vice versa, which means that the equilibrium is due among other things to a reinforcement of the differentiation and the integration. Consequently, if there is an outside disturbance, stemming, for example, from a substitution of B'' for B', either the conservation of the whole becomes impossible and the organism dies (if we referred to a cognitive system, we would say the substitution would be rejected), or there is a compensating modification (B is modified into B_2 which remains inserted in the cycle) and adaptation with survival for an organism or new equilibrium for a cognitive system (with the possibility that the earlier system remains valid as a substructure for the category of objects B' and produces a new substructure for the objects B'').

But the difference between the biological and cognitive systems is that the first does not reach the elaboration of forms without exogenous contents. In other words, the mutual conservation of the elements of the cycle A, B, C, etc., is not possible without their continuously being fed by means of outside elements A', B', C', etc. If most of the cognitive systems apply to reality, their forms, A, B, C, etc., also assimilate an outside content, A', B', C', etc.; on the other hand, there are formal systems in which, given thematized objects of thought, the subject merely considers

[3] For example, we might have two subsystems AM and NZ or KZ each forming a cycle but coordinated to each other with or without interaction and subordinated to the whole cycle.

the first elements of a structure without supplying it with outside contents. For example, a child aged seven or eight will spontaneously use the sections of a double entry chart to classify the four categories of red and white squares and circles, thus forming a cycle of interdependent formal elements, A, B, C, D, but applied to the objects A', B', C', D', whereas a logician or a mathematician constructing the theory of the Cartesian product would merely turn to the attributes to free the algebraic characteristics. Likewise, it goes without saying, that on the level of the sensorimotor schemes, the various movements and constitutive perceptive indications of a scheme will be linked, in a cycle of elements in interaction ABC, etc., inseparably to the material content of the actions and their objectives, i.e., A', B', C', etc., whereas a similar scheme (for example, a group of displacements), when expressed much later in operations, can give rise to purely formal considerations.

Let us again remember that such epistemic cycles and their functioning are due to two fundamental processes which form the components of any cognitive equilibrium.

The first is the assimilation or incorporation of an outside element (object, event, and so forth) into the subject's sensorimotor or conceptual scheme. Thus it is a question of the relation between the A' B' C' . . . and the ABC . . . , although we can also speak of reciprocal assimilation when two schemes or two subsystems (for example, looking and seizing) are applied to the same objects or coordinate without having further need of the actual content. We can even consider as a reciprocal assimilation the relations between a total system, characterized by its own laws of composition, and the subsystems which it includes with their differentiations, for the subsystems' integration into a whole is an assimilation to a common structure, and the differentiations include assimilations which occur according to special conditions but are deducible from possible variations of the whole.

The second central process is the accommodation that is the result of the necessity to consider the particularities characteristic of the elements that are to be assimilated. In the relations between the *ABC* . . . and the *A'B'C'* . . . the differentiations due to the accommodation speak for themselves; the scheme to grasp, for example, does not apply in the same manner to very small and to very large objects. But here again, it is worthwhile to generalize this process to the relations between the subsystems and those which unite their differentiation and to integrate them into a single whole. If the reciprocal assimilations are not accompanied by accommodations that are also reciprocal, there will be a distorted merger and no coordination between the systems to be linked. For example, the synthesis of numerical and spatial structures, the basis of our number system, assumes the partition of the content into units yet doesn't abolish the continuity. But it is clear that if the accommodation is constantly subordinated to the assimilation (for it is always the accommodation of a scheme of assimilation), this accommodation is smaller and above all more foreseeable in the case of these reciprocal accommodations than when new "observables" and adaptations must be made to the outside objects *A'B'C'.* . . .

Thus in order to develop a theory of equilibration, it is necessary at the outset to consider the two postulates which arise from our research on reflective abstraction.[4]

First postulate: Any scheme of assimilation tends to feed itself, that is, to incorporate outside elements compatible with its nature into itself. This postulate assigns a driving force to the process and therefore must assume activity on the part of the subject, but by itself it does not imply the construction of novelties; a rather large scheme (such as that of "existence") could assimilate the entire universe without being modified or enriching itself in compensation.

Second postulate: The entire scheme of assimilation must alter as it accommodates to the elements it assimilates; that is, it modifies itself in relation to the particularities of events

---

[4] We speak of postulates in the sense of general propositions derived from the study of facts.

but does not lose its continuity (hence it can maintain closure and function as a cycle of interdependent processes) nor its earlier powers of assimilation. This second postulate (already proved valid on the biological level by the formation of phenotypical "accommodates") states the necessity for an equilibrium between the assimilation and the accommodation in order for the accommodation to succeed and remain compatible with the cycle, modified or not. But although we can thus express the possibility of cycle modifications, we cannot foresee their nature; accommodations may be to exterior objects or to other schemes (during reciprocal assimilations) and the resultant changes can be exogenous or endogenous and include very variable parts of transformations.

Let us note that if the second postulate requires the formation of an equilibrium between the assimilation and the accommodation, this implies nothing more than: (1) the necessity for accommodations in the cycle structures and (2) the conservation of such structures when there are successful accommodations. We thus remain on the level of description and do not interpret the meaning of these equilibriums or the eventual regulations and compensations which could be used in these equilibriums. The cognitive equilibrium has until now been characterized merely by mutual conservations. To attribute these conservations to assimilation (postulate 1) and the additional processes of accommodation (postulate 2) does not constitute a theory about structural methods of cognition, for these two notions depend solely on functional description.

§2/   *The Three Forms of Equilibration and the Relation between Negations and Affirmations*

A consideration of the cycles described in §1 shows at once the necessity for three kinds of equilibrations and holds us to a first approximation of a definition of mutual conservations.

1. At the beginning of the fundamental interaction of the subject and the objects, there is the equilibration between the assimilation of schemes of action and the accommodation of these to the objects. Let us note that here there is the beginning of mutual conservation, for the object is necessary to the development of the action and vice versa; it is the scheme of assimilation which confers its significance to the object and transforms it by displacement, use, or other action. Assimilation and accommodation (when successful) then form a whole in which the two aspects A and A' (or B and B', etc.) imply one another; however, in case of failure they correspond to two factors of contrary meaning which leads to abandonment of the action.

2. An equilibration results from the interactions between the subsystems. Now, from the very beginning, the equilibration is far from being automatic or given, for the subsystems can depend on schemes which at first are independent. Actually, the incorporation into a scheme of all the elements which feed it, as described in postulate 1 of §1, simply occurs progressively; this is especially evident given reciprocal assimilations. Moreover, the subsystems are generally constructed at different speeds, i.e., with temporal lags of greater or lesser importance; hence, there are causes here for possible nonbalance and the impetus to reach an equilibration. Nevertheless, although the accommodation of schemes to the outer reality is interrupted by many unexpected obstacles, the reciprocal assimilation of two valid subsystems and their reciprocal accommodation succeed sooner or later and lead to mutual conservation.

3. Furthermore we must consider separately the progressive equilibrium between the differentiation and the integration, i.e., relations uniting subsystems to the totality which includes them. This third form of equilibration does not merge with the second, since it involves a hierarchy and not only the simple relationships between collaterals. In fact, a totality is characterized by its particular laws of composition, which determine a cycle of interdependent operations and are superior in rank to the special characteristics of

subsystems. Consider, for example, the following synthesis of two subsystems into a totality: the exterior referential is to a moving form such as a train and the interior referential is to a traveler walking about in the moving train. The totality includes laws of composition other than those evoked by the subsystems (displacement concepts describing only horizontal movement). In this example, the integration into a whole is a matter of assimilation, and the differentiation requires accommodations. Nevertheless, there is a mutual conservation of the whole and of the parts, and in this sense reciprocal assimilations and accommodations take place according to a hierarchy and are not influenced only by collateral relationships.

The three kinds of equilibrations which we have just distinguished all involve equilibrium between assimilation and accommodation, and deal only with the positive characteristics belonging to schemes, subsystems, or totalities; even when structures have reverse operations, they show characteristics like the others and are in this sense positive. But we must add that the equilibration of each structure includes a certain relationship—the nature of which may be determined—between positive and negative characteristics, and these characteristics are necessary to delimit positive characteristics. An understanding of this concept is essential to our discussion.

(1). In the equilibration between the schemes of the subject, A, B, or C, etc., and the exterior objects, A', B', etc., the subject's actions, forecasts, judgments, and so forth, must not only possess certain characteristics a', but the subject must also distinguish these characteristics from different characteristics, x, y, etc., considered as *non-a'*. Likewise, in order to use, judge, or classify A' with characteristics a', we must turn to the scheme A and not to others considered *non-A*. It is evident therefore that any term, in extension as in comprehension, is opposed to any others, which infers processing as many negations as affirmations; this relationship can remain implicit, but it often requires a more or less systematic delineation.

It constantly happens that a scheme A does not find its ordinary aliments A' but can accommodate itself to terms A'' with neighboring characteristics a''. If this accommodation succeeds, scheme A gives rise to a modification A_2, but this novelty does not abolish the existence of A which we can also denote as A_1. The initial scheme A then includes the presence of two subschemes, A_1 and A_2, hence, $A = A_1 + A_2$. However, if this subdivision is to be stabilized in a balanced form (A_2 using merely the A'' and A_1 the A') the partial negations $A_2 = A \cdot non\text{-}A_1$ and $A_1 = A \cdot non\text{-}A_2$ are indispensable (and are constituents of the secondary categories of the groupings, hence complementaries under the closest interlocking category). We thus see the functional necessary of negations.

(2). Consider the equilibration by reciprocal assimilation and accommodation of two subsystems, S_1 and S_2. A structure of intersection when added requires negations. Actually, to coordinate the two subsystems, S_1 and S_2, is to discover a common operative part, $S_1 \cdot S_2$, which is opposed to $S_1 \cdot non\text{-}S_2$ and to $S_2 \cdot non\text{-}S_1$; hence, we see that partial negations are indispensable to the coherent stability of this coordination.

(3). In the equilibration of the integration and the differentiation, the necessity for negations is equally clear. On the one hand, to differentiate a totality, T, in subsystems, S, means not only to confirm what each of these possesses but also to exclude, or deny, the characteristics each system does not have. On the other hand, to form (to integrate) a total system, T, means to free positively the characteristics common to all the S, but this also means to distinguish—this time negatively—the common features of special characteristics not belonging to T. In short, the differentiation is based on negations and then, in turn, the integration implies them. The totality T is modified and remains superior in rank to S, but within a new enlarged totality.

The three kinds of equilibrations as the products of progressive assimilation and accommodation (postulates 1 and 2) can be accomplished in a spontaneous and intuitive manner by successive groupings, which eliminate failures and retain success; but insofar as the subject seeks an adjustment—tends to obtain a coherent stability—he must use the exclusions in a systematic manner. Only an exact relationship between affirmations and negations ensures the equilibrium.

§3/   *The Reason for the Occurrence of Nonbalance and Its Initial Frequency*

These purely descriptive remarks raise the primary problem of any theory of equilibration: if the significance of cognitive "good forms" and the required characteristic of the equilibrium are not given from the very beginning, nor with the same force at every level, why are there instances of nonbalance? And are these periods inevitable? Actually it is clear that one of the sources of progress in the development of knowledge is to be found in nonbalance as such which alone can force a subject to go beyond his present state and to seek new equilibriums. However, it is equally evident that, if nonbalance is an essential motivational factor, nevertheless it cannot succeed in giving rise to the content required for specific reequilibrations. But we may ask if nonbalance is inherent in the subject's very actions or merely due to contingent historical situations. A question arises therefore of establishing whether the cases of nonbalance, in other words the contradictions, are inherent in the constitution of the objects on the one hand, or in the subject's actions on the other.

We may ask, furthermore, if they result merely from momentary conflicts which we may assume occur in any historical development. In this case, they would simply be due to systems and subsystems of observation and coordination, because none of the systems can be completed immediately (causal systems are never finished) and they develop at different speeds. In short, no form of thought, at any level, is capable of becoming instantaneously a coherent, total reality.

It is worthwhile to note that however the nonbalance arises, it produces the driving force of development. Without this, knowledge remains static. But nonbalance also plays a release role, since its fecundity is measured by the possibility of surmounting it, in other words, of reaching a higher equilibrium. It is therefore evident that the real source of progress is to be sought in both the insufficiency responsible for the conflict and the improvement expressed in the equilibration. Without the nonbalance there would not be "increasing reequilibration." (Reequilibration expresses the obtained improvement.)

The full significance of progressive equilibration as a process of development should not be underestimated in favor of that of nonbalance. The "dialectics of nature" has attempted with some exaggeration to find "contradictions" in the very heart of operations at play in the physical world, for example, in situations of actions and reactions; these causal models are in fact exempt of any logical or normative contradiction.[5] In the biological field, on the other hand, it would appear that possible disturbances, defined as "normal" and "abnormal" ("normative" or "not normative" in the cognitive sense), speak in favor of inherent nonbalance expressed in the very laws of life (for example, death is not the reverse operation of survival as is the dissociation of a molecule as compared to the intact molecule). In the sociological field Marxist dialectics insist on the fundamental role of conflict and nonbalance, but we are not competent to

[5] It is true we speak of contradiction or disturbance of a physical nature and the reasons for the irreversibility of certain phenomena. But, if we refer to the increasing probability of mixtures of interference between independent causal series (in the Cournot sense), the disorders as such would be interpreted as caused by operations which are by no means contradictory but those of probability: statistic causality is the result of logico-mathematical operations attributed to reality in a manner exempt of any contradiction.

judge this theory. In describing cognitive development, the proposition that nonbalance or contradictions are inherent in the very characteristics of thought seems difficult to support, at least in the present state of our knowledge. We have not succeeded in supplying a formal elaboration of a "logic" dialectic; "contradiction," consequently, appears as a notion whose significance is psychogenetic, sociogenetic, or historical, and not inherent in the operational structures which lead to a state of closure.[6]

But if nonbalance and contradictions are not inherent in formal structures of a subject's logic, can we look for them in prelogic or preoperational levels? If defects of equilibrium, as we just suggested, depend on the difficulties of adjustment between subject and objects or on coordination between the subsystems and between the differentiation and the integration, do the initial stages of the psychology of thought, rather than its logical structure, explain the slow construction of logic and the obstacles it encounters? Actually, if we limit ourselves to what we previously called historical contingencies, we can understand the existence of momentary nonbalance, but by no means do we explain why periods of nonbalance would be more numerous at the elementary stages than afterward. At every level (including those of scientific thought) new effects occur between the subject and the objects, and between the subsystems (cf. those of micro- and macrophysics), but these initial effects often pose particularly serious problems of integration (e.g., consider the history of the unit number system).

The historical or psychogenetic occasions of conflict are far more frequent at the initial stages and nonbalance is far more difficult to overcome. There must be a reason for this, and it cannot depend on the nature of the problems encountered, since elementary and simple questions should

[6] This in no way prevents the presentation of the development of logical ideas in dialectic form, as shown by Greniewski at one of our symposiums, when the historical development of logic, and not logic itself, was described.

correspond to conflicts which are also simple. The explanation must have general application and depend on the subject's reasoning methods (or "strategies"—if we choose to use a more fashionable term) rather than on the contents of the reasoning.

The answer follows from the preceding remarks on negation and our previous research on contradiction; because the mind spontaneously concentrates on the affirmations and positive characteristics of the objects, actions, or even operations, the negations are neglected or are constructed only secondarily and laboriously. Since they are required for every form of equilibration (see §2), they are achieved only after multiple difficulties and their elaboration requires long periods of time. We have no need, therefore, to postulate activity to produce the existence of initial profound nonbalance, as we postulate the necessity of an equilibrium by mutual conservations between differentiated elements. Nonbalance at the beginning is a fact, and since the search for coherence is another (which logic expresses normatively), we must explain the passage from the first to the second, which is the proper task of a theory of equilibration. But before continuing this discussion, we again state why the construction of negations raises problems for the subject.

First, let us recall that in mathematical logic the question of negation is far from being solved.[7] If we use a classical definition of negation, we neglect the linguistic difference between the rejection of a proposition and the acceptance of its negative. If, as in the system of logic known as "natural," we define *non-p* by "*p* implies *f*" where *f* is a false statement, either there are as many negations as false statements, or we consider all of them equivalences which is more natural. In the Griss and Nelson systems negation is defined as a simple difference. From the psychological viewpoint there is a very notable distinction, and from the

---

[7] My thanks to L. Apostel for his observations on the subject.

viewpoint of logic a difference presupposes a negation. For our purposes a model would need a quantifier whose variation would cover the entire field.

Here we will limit ourselves to linking negation with reversibility and using the quantifiers "all," "a few," "one," and "none." Hence $non\text{-}p = O,p$, by identity of the negation, $p \cdot (non\text{-}p) = O$, the refusal but with inversion, and $non(non\text{-}p) = p$. Or if P is the category of the true values of p, its cancellation (an empty category) gives $P - P = O$. These formulations tie up with the principal proposition of our work on contradiction according to which contradiction is conceived as an incomplete compensation, $p \cdot (non\text{-}p) > O$.

From the psychological viewpoint, let us recall (see *Recherches sur la contradiction*) that negation is essential only when the subject has no need to construct it, i.e., when it is imposed from without. For example, a denial of the facts is a reply to a false forecast (or actually a refusal to accept what is unwanted). When there is a failure in object accommodation, in order to understand the reasons for the failure and to change this into success, we must distinguish the positive characteristics a from their absence $non\text{-}a$ with justification of this negation. As for scheme A used during a forecast, it is important to dissociate A from subsequent schemes A_1 and A_2, whether a is given or not. In short, we must substitute a category B and its subcategories for A_1 and A_2 so that each includes its positive characteristics, and also the negation of the others. Our research on consciousness and on success and understanding as well as on contradiction revealed to us the slow formation of these constructions; they occur only when an adjustment of quantifications ($B = A_1 + A_2$ signifies "all the A_1 are B but only a few B are A_1") which are bound up with the reversibility ($B - A_2 = A_1$, etc.) and are the operational result of the coordination of negations and of positive operations (which begin with seven- or eight-year-olds) to find this elaboration of negations. The same is true *a fortiori* for the coordinations between subsystems and those of differentiations and integrations. All negations are constructed by the subject and by no means result from object resistance. This construction is slower and more difficult than the more or less direct composition of positive characteristics.

We do not have to argue about the primacy of affirmations. We record only positive observations, and the perception of the absence of an object only occurs secondarily and in waiting periods or forecasts which depend on the whole action and extend beyond the perception.

When speaking of actions we should remember these are centered on the aim to be reached and not on the distance to be covered. Generally speaking, displacements are first conceived relative to the point of arrival rather than to the space left empty by the moving body (hence the well-known errors concerning, for example, the nonconservation of lengths). The conceptualizations begin with an organization of the positive characteristics—and language itself eloquently reveals traces of it: "more or less heavy" means any weight; whereas "more or less light" (which logically is the exact equivalent, but in negative terms) merely refers to inferior values. In brief, everything is aimed at the primacy of the positive during the elementary stages, and the positive corresponds to what, on the level of experience, represents the "immediate data," whereas negation depends either on derived verifications or on more or less labored constructions as determined by the complexity of the systems.

We see that equilibration in its various forms appears to constitute the fundamental factor of cognitive development. We note that during the initial periods of cognition the asymmetry of the affirmations and negations causes nonbalance which compromises the equilibrium between the subject and the objects, between the subsystems, and between the total system and the parts.

To summarize: the progressive equilibration is an indispensable process in development and a process whose manifestations show modifications from stage to stage. The successive equilibriums show improvement in their qualitative structure in their field of application, in the construction and refinement of negations, and in the quantifications they assume. Furthermore, the various coordinations dissussed in §2 are specified and consolidated. The role of negations will be discussed later in an attempt to isolate the mechanism of equilibration, starting with a first approximation of a mutual conservation and an analysis of regulations and compensations.

§4/   The Regulations

We have admitted as facts of observation the existence of several forms of equilibrium but have characterized them by their particular mutual conservations, so that we have merely given a description and not an explanation. We will now explore the "how" of equilibration and reequilibration by turning to the processes of regulation.

1. In general we speak of regulation when the reaction, A', of an action, A, is modified by the original action, i.e., there is a secondary effect of A on the new development A'. The regulation can then be seen as a correction by A (negative feedback) or reinforcement (positive feedback). However, we must specify the varieties of disturbances and underline the fact that the inverse relationship is not true; that is, all disturbances do not create regulations (hence equilibrations).

We must distinguish two important categories of disturbances. The first includes those which are opposed to accommodations: resistance of objects, obstacles to reciprocal assimilations of schemes or subsystems, etc. In short, these are the reasons for failures or errors of which the subject becomes more or less aware; the corresponding regulations include negative feedback. The second category of disturbances, the source of nonbalance, consists of gaps which leave requirements unfulfilled and are expressed by the insufficiency of a scheme. But it is worth stressing—and this is essential—that all gaps do not constitute disturbances;

for example, a scientist is by no means motivated by the considerable field of his ignorance (gap in his knowledge) because most questions do not concern him. On the other hand, a gap becomes a disturbance when it indicates the absence of an object, the lack of conditions necessary to accomplish an action, or want of knowledge that is indispensable in solving a problem. The gap, functioning as a disturbance, is therefore always defined by an already activated scheme of assimilation, and the corresponding regulation then includes a positive feedback which prolongs the assimilating activity of this scheme (postulate 1 of §1).

Although it is important to remember that any regulation is a reaction to a disturbance, the opposite can be verified only partially. We cannot speak of regulation (a) when the disturbance simply creates a repetition of the action with no modification and with the illusory hope of improvement (as is often the case with the child); (b) when the obstacle leads to the end of action; or (c) when the subject, interested by an unexpected aspect of the disturbance, engages his activity in another direction. It is evident that in these situations we cannot speak of a modification of A' caused by A's reaction to A', and in the absence of this regulation there is no reequilibration. In other words, if regulation is to occur, a regulator must intervene, and we must discover its nature. Before doing so, however, let us study the various varieties of regulations.

2. First, let us note that the classic duality of positive and negative feedback actually exists only when analysis can isolate sections of a total behavior. Analysis can identify the formation of a structure in which positive and negative feedback occur. The first consists of reinforcements and the second of corrections. In general, these two processes are required for the functioning of a behavior however complex. For example, acquiring a habit is currently assumed to use positive feedback, but it goes without saying that in addition the activity implies much groping which depends on negative feedback. In this example as in many others, reinforcements and corrections are constantly added.

On the other hand, seen in its entirety, a dichotomy concerning behavior is the result of regulations attempting to conserve a state and intervening in the progression to a new state. In biological terms we speak of homeostasis and homeorhesis (the latter is influenced by the mixture just discussed of positive and negative feedback).

Another essential dichotomy concerns the regulations of the subject's relationships with the objects to which he must adapt himself (assimilation and accommodation aiming at the physical or noetic possession of these objects) and of the relationships between schemes or between scheme systems (subsystems of the entire instruments of action or of thought available to the subject at his level). In fact, these relationships, which result in reciprocal assimilations and accommodations, do not always succeed at once, even if each of the subsystems is coherent in itself. Inhelder, Sinclair, and Bovet have furnished fine examples of these conflicts in their studies on cognitive experience.[8] Thus the comparison of two lengths, represented by small rods aligned end to end, can give rise to durable conflicts if the lengths are evaluated both spatially and by the number of units in each (especially if the units are not all equal). In this situation there is a need for linking the subsystems or modifying them sufficiently to resolve the conflicts or contradictions, and it goes without saying that many regulations are required. The immediate relationships between the subject and objects serve merely as support for more complex relationships which are developed through subsystems between them. In other words, the problems arise not from empirical abstractions but from pseudoempirical abstractions (that is, from characteristics which the subject's operations introduce into the objects, such as order and number, and not from the physical characteristics). We can see that this is a more complex type of regulation.

A third dichotomy deals with the means and serves both

[8] B. Inhelder, H. Sinclair, and M. Bovet, *Apprentissage et structures de la connaissance*, Presses Universitaires de France, 1974.

almost automatic regulations and active (more conscious) adjustments. The first are found in simple sensorimotor performances which are subjected to slight variations (for example the attempt to seize an object by considering distances and size dictates a greater or smaller opening of the hands and extension of the arm). We will speak of active adjustment when a subject is led to change means or can hesitate (for example, when a child builds a card house) indicating the intervention thereby of a need to make choices. Although it is difficult to draw a boundary between the two categories, their separation is important because the automatic regulations function with little awareness, whereas the active adjustments create the regulations and are therefore at the source of a representation or conceptualization of the physical actions. This will lead to a subordination of the regulations of the physical actions to a superior control. Here we have the beginning of regulation at a second level.

Hence we predicate a hierarchy of regulations and can classify them accordingly: there are simple regulations, regulations of regulations, etc., up to self-regulations with self-organization which are capable of modifying and enriching the initial program by differentiation, multiplication, coordination of the goals, and integration of subsystems into a whole system. We will return to this in §6.

Let us review. Obviously we could classify the regulations according to other criteria, for example, according to their contents (regulation of observations, coordinations, etc.). However, a hierarchical classification is more significant. The regulations which adjust the recording of observations actually help adapt a form to a material content (that is, help to assimilate an observation to a concept, and the result of the regulations is the construction of new forms on this first-degree level. Then we have the regulation of regulations, and finally the self-organization with equilibriums of differentiations and integrations.

3. We now face the fundamental problem of the regulator(s), for a regulation suggests a programmed control as

in a machine (e.g., a thermostat). The subject first identifies characteristics of objects to which he is related asymptotically. We have shown elsewhere[9] that this empirical abstraction is possible at every level only because of the assimilating limits (e.g., the logico-mathematical instruments the physicist uses to not only state laws but also record facts) which are taken from the subject's action coordinations by reflective abstraction. As for the logico-mathematical structures in general, it would be inconceivable to attribute to them, as regulators, the physical nature of objects, since they extend beyond them everywhere. If a harmony exists between mathematics and reality, it is because of the subject's operations. Indeed the organism is one of many physical objects of reality but it is more active than the others which explains both the harmony and the going beyond the logico-mathematical structures.

Thus the only regulator we could assign to the cognitive regulations is an internal one. As their program is not hereditary, their existence can be attributed to the mutual conservations inherent in the functional process of the assimilation. This interpretation might appear as a disturbing vicious circle, since the cycle of interactions would thus be both the cause and the result of regulations. But in dealing with any biological or cognitive system, we must characterize the whole as primordial and not proceed from the assembled parts or the differentiations based on the assembling. Hence, the whole possesses a force of cohesion and therefore characteristics of self-conservation which distinguish it from nonorganic physical-chemical totalities. Le Dantec, who certainly was no vitalist, said that in distinction to chemical reactions, where the compositions of two compounds are destroyed or modified during the production of new ones, the characteristic reactions of organisms that are assimilating can be written $A + A = \lambda A + A''$ where A is the substance of the organism, A' the integrated substances,

---

[9] See our study, *L'abstraction réfléchissante*, soon to be published.

A'' the rejected substances, and $\lambda > 1$. We can use this expression with our usual symbolism if A is a cognitive system, A' the objects which feed it, and A'' the objects it does not assimilate.

This equation shows the conservation of the whole as such—the conservation of its structure during assimilation instead of its modification by the assimilated elements. It is a significant fact that in all vital and cognitive fields the total form appears more stable than its components. Not only does an organism maintain its own form despite a continual metabolism, but, as P. Weiss has noted in discussing the cell, the total behavior "is infinitely less variable from one instant to another than the momentary activity of its elements."[10] In any cognitive system the laws governing the whole override the changing characteristics of the components. Pressburger, mentioned by Tarski, has even shown for totalities the existence of complete and entirely predictable systems, although their subsystems function in a partially unpredictable manner. Let us also remember that in mathematics "a more 'general' theory which 'contains' less general theories explains them to a greater degree than if they were taken in an isolated manner or together."[11]

Thus there is no circle (or more precisely it exists but has nothing vicious about it) predicated when we admit that a whole system plays the role of regulator for the subsystems, for it imposes on them an extremely restrained standard: to submit themselves to the conservation of the whole, i.e., to the closing of an interaction cycle, or be carried off in a general dislocation comparable to the death of an organism. Just as the continual play of assimilations and accommodations constantly causes reinforcements and corrections, so both take the form of regulations or feedback the moment

---

[10] See P. Weiss, *The Living System, Beyond Reductionism* (Alpbach Symposium, 1968), London, Hutchinson, 1969, p. 12.

[11] G. Henriques, *L'explication dans les sciences*, Paris, Flammarion, 1973, Chapter 11.

they extend (and the assimilating method forces them) into "retroactive" and "proactive" processes, but they remain under the permanent dynamic control of the whole which requires its own conservation. Certainly this is merely a functional programming yet it adapts itself to every situation.

4. Let us return to the question of affirmations and negations. We should mention that the subject is not aware of the important role these regulations play. Any regulation by its very nature can cause two processes, functioning in opposite directions, to intervene: the one "retroactive," leading from the results of an action back to its starting point, and the other "proactive," leading to a correction or to a reinforcement. These two movements in opposite directions do not yet constitute direct and opposite operations, since their courses differ. Therefore we rightly qualify them as "loops," but with respect to their orientations the one is very much the negation of the other; here there are activities leading toward reversibility. But it is above all in their teleology that the negations intervene. The negative feedback, as its name implies, consists of a correction that is suppressive whether it is a question of removing obstacles, of modifying the schemes by eliminating one movement for the benefit of another, or of decreasing a force of its extension, etc. Positive feedback is a reinforcement and in this sense seems opposed to any negation. But where it differs in the cognitive field from other assimilating activity which aims to generalize its feeding (postulate 1, §1) is precisely in that it tends to reinforce by filling a gap (or bolstering a weakness) in its attempt to reach or to stabilize a goal. A gap is a negative characteristic and to fill a gap by a reinforcement is again a suppression, but it deals with an insufficiency as such. Thus we are not merely playing with words when we say we see in positive feedback the negation of a negation; an example would be the removal of the space-time distance which prevents the attainment of a goal.

One more remark on the constructive characteristic of regulations. On the one hand, almost all regulations lead finally to compensations, as we are about to see. On the other hand, these compensations are inseparable from a construction problem. In fact, either the regulation passes beyond the initial action in the direction of a greater and more stable equilibrium, in which case the equilibration is increasing, or else it limits itself to stabilizing the initial action and at the same time adding to it new "retroactive" and "proactive" circuits. Furthermore, the regulations increase the power of negations—which is lacking at the initial levels—and thus this also constitutes progress in equilibration, since the initial nonbalance is essentially due to a deficit of negative characteristics (see §3).

§5/ *The Compensations*

In order to formulate a theory explaining the development of cognitive structures by equilibration one must obviously consider the final reversibility of logico-mathematical operations (inversion and reciprocity) by methods which do not presuppose it but which lead to it in successive stages. It must be the necessary result of psychogenetic constructions yet conform to a timeless and general standard. To achieve this goal, two conditions must be fulfilled: the reversibility must be shown to be the product of compensation systems of different levels, and the reason why these compensations are inseparable from constructions proper must be discovered. We know that any new construction is not only inseparable from compensations or complements but also directed by their requirements.

1. Our next step is to establish what the regulations consist of when they finally produce compensations. But let us first note that if any reaction to a disturbance (obstacle or gap) does not produce a regulation (the regulation intervening only under the pressure of a whole system), neither does any regulation produce a compensation. An exception, however, appears when certain positive feedback leads to a reinforcement of an error. But in the cognitive field this

exception exists only momentarily; sooner or later the error leads to contradictions and, as we have seen elsewhere,[12] these contradictions consist of incomplete compensations $(a \times non\text{-}a \neq O)$.

If we call compensation an action in a direction opposite to a given effect which thus tends to cancel or to neutralize the effect, it is obvious that the negative feedback plays just such a role as an instrument of correction. When it is a question of correcting the action itself, these types of driving negations are evident. Consider behavior at the start of a bicycle ride: straightening oneself to compensate for slopes that could lead to a fall or bending at a turn when a vertical position might threaten balance. As for outside obstacles, these are avoided, which means compensating for the disturbances by a whole or partial negation, the latter corresponding to a differentiation of the scheme into subschemes which determine whether or not the goal can be attained by a direct itinerary.

Likewise, if we must make representative assimilations— and no longer only sensorimotor—because of disturbances created by objects that can't be assimilated by means of available schemes or by facts that contradict forecasts, we again find similar varieties: either the outside event is denied as a disturbance (by negligence or often even by a kind of repression), or there is a modification of schemes and hence differentiation in subschemes with the partial negations they include. In any case there is a compensation (but with more or less stability).

In general, regulations by negative feedback lead finally to compensations. Within these we can distinguish two categories: the compensations by "inversion," which are cancellations of the disturbance, and the compensations by "reciprocity," which are modifications of the scheme to accommodate it to the initially disturbing element. The first therefore imply whole negations, and the second partial negations, but these occur within the new system thus re-

---

[12] See our *Recherches sur la contradiction.*

organized. In the case of disturbances which occur during the reciprocal assimilations of schemes or of subsystems, it goes without saying that the regulations result in compensations by reciprocity.

2. The situation for positive feedback appears more complex yet by no means is the possibility of reaching compensations excluded (except when there is momentary error reinforcement)—if it were, we would fail to understand why there are regulations. First, let us recall the essential fact that the acquisition of any behavior where reinforcements are involved implies corrections; if reinforcements are useless, the reason is that there is immediate success or comprehension. Turning to reinforcements implies the presence of difficulties and hence corrections. This means that positive feedback in general is linked to negatives and to the compensations they include. This is especially evident in what we called in §4 the "active adjustments," for to change means is due both to reinforcement and correction. But let us remember that reinforcement due to the positive feedback is meant to fill a gap (as when there is insufficient power for an action, too great a space-time distance separating the subject from a goal, etc.). To fill a gap is a compensation according to our definition (we thus avoid returning to the double negation). But this is not yet the essential element: the principal factor, during the formation of a positive feedback, is the value that the subject attributes to the pursued goal which makes him judge as indispensable the corresponding satisfaction (physical or purely cognitive).

Every author who has studied requirements, especially that pure functionalist Claparède (and he fully recognized the relations between the requirements in general and the "question" for initial movement and the necessity of the act of intelligence), has presented the requirement as a momentary nonbalance and its satisfaction as a reequilibration. It is sufficient to say that the reinforcement (regardless of its positive characteristic) plays a role of compensation—one can compare it to a deficit in a "budget" (to speak like that

other functionalist Janet) without which the budget would
end up negative.

In §27 we will return to the problem of the choice of
goals in relation to the reciprocal assimilation of subsystems
and above all to the equilibrium of the differentiations and
the integration, and we will see that this choice is conditioned by compensation requirements. This observation
raises the problem of the regulations of regulations. Here
again, if a regulation is insufficient, that is, if it fails to
cancel all the disturbances or to fill the gaps, it will become
necessary to subordinate it to others which play a double
role of correction and reinforcement. We then are faced
with the same questions and similar compensations, and
once again we must explain the possibility of such improvement (see §6). But as the compensations in play are more
complex—since here they deal with methods already functioning as compensators—the negations they produce are
also of a more elaborate type and begin to appear as opposite operations. The negative aspects of the elementary
compensations cannot be easily apprehended by the subject's consciousness insofar as he reasons in terms of simple
differences—he is likely to do so in making "comprehension" judgments; and a long road is traveled before operational negations or contrary operations are dealt with. The
compensations characteristic of the regulations of regulations are distinguished by the fact that instead of being
opposed to disturbances that are initially external, they deal
increasingly with internal activity.

3. Let us now study the characteristics common to these
various regulating compensations. The first has been described above. We repeat: all compensation works in an
opposite or reciprocal direction to that of the disturbance
(obstacle or gap), which means it either cancels (inversion)
or neutralizes the disturbance (reciprocity), while gaining
useful information (we will discuss this in §6) in addition
to developing the negations which are involved, level by
level, in the disturbance-compensation pairs.

The second general characteristic of the cognitive compensations is that they include a terminal evaluation of their success or insufficiency which is linked to the source of the regulation itself. Since this source consists of a nonbalance of the assimilation and of the accommodation, the final evaluation involves a judgment dealing with success (whole, partial, or missing). First there is the assimilation of data, and afterward there is the possibility of the comprehension of new relations owing to the reequilibration of the assimilation and the accommodation, and to information taken from initially disturbing elements and finally integrated into the readapted behavior (we will return to this in §13).

The third characteristic common to every compensation is the tendency to conservations through transformations, i.e., conservation of a state or of a progression, of a scheme or of a subsystem, etc. These preserving tendencies do not result at once in the construction of notions or structural principles of conservation (substance, etc.), for to reach this point, the compensations must be qualified; but in their initial qualified form, these compensations from the very outset furnish functional outlines for later performances, just as the negations which they imply at every level prepare for the contrary operations equally necessary to the operational conservations.

A final remark is necessary. Although the regulations and the compensations which they create use the equilibration method, it is important to emphasize the fact that these formative processes are both constructive and preservative. In itself a regulation is a construction, since it adds "retroactions" or paths in loops to the linear course of an action. Even if the result is merely to stabilize the action, there is, nevertheless, enrichment through the construction of new relations which include among others the formation of implicit negations. In more general terms, the introduction of disturbing elements, and the accommodations resulting from compensations, produce new knowledge, some relative to the objects and some to the subject's very actions, in such a manner that the reequilibration becomes inseparable from the constructions; and these constructions are formed in part by the anticipatory power which sooner or later results from "retroactions."

§6/ The Increasing Equilibration

The study of regulations has shown us how equilibration is achieved in its three forms: between the subject and the objects, between schemes or subschemes on the same hierarchic level, and between their differentiations and their integrations into superior totalities. We must stress that cognitive equilibration never reaches a stopping point, even on a temporary basis, and that this situation is not to be regretted; and to top it off we see no indication of a kind of original sin in contradiction as certain dialectics would like to see installed in the very heart of intelligence. The fact that states of equilibrium are always exceeded is the result, on the contrary, of a very positive force. Any knowledge raises new problems as it solves preceding ones. This is evident in the experimental sciences where the discovery of the causality of a phenomenon raises the question of the cause of the causality and so forth. And this even describes the situation in the logico-mathematical fields where equilibriums are at their most stable, since a truth acquired by mathematical demonstration is kept indefinitely. By no means does an equilibrium constitute a stopping point, since any finished structure can always give rise to new requirements in fresh substructures or to integrations in greater structures. The reason for this necessity to improve any cognitive equilibrium is that the process of equilibration intrinsically involves the necessity to construct; hence, there is always excess construction and a certain stabilizing conservation exists only within transformations. Briefly, compensation and construction are always inseparable.

To review: a system never constitutes an absolute end of a process of equilibration; fresh goals always arise from an attained equilibrium, unstable or even stable; and each result, even if more or less durable, remains pregnant with new progress. To conceive of equilibration as a mere step to equilibrium would, therefore, be inadequate, since in addition to being a means of structuring, it is constantly attempting to achieve a *better* equilibrium. No balanced structure can be said to remain in a final state even if it is found to conserve its special characteristics without modifications. That is why, in addition to simple equilibrations, always limited and incomplete, we speak of *increasing equilibrations* in the sense of these improved states, and we can even speak of a law of optimalization if this term does not imply a technical quantitative significance.

This increase is attained in two ways: the improvements may result simply from the success of compensating regulations, hence from momentarily attained equilibrium, or from novelties (from reflective abstractions) arising out of the very method of these regulations. In fact, any regulation adds new transformations to the system to be adjusted, and these transformations have their own structure which can enrich the system that is being balanced.

1. Among the effects of the improved equilibrations in the first category is extension; insofar as the disturbing elements are assimilated to the scheme, the scheme is increased. In our *Recherches sur la contradiction*, we noted that enlargement is accompanied (as condition or effect) by a referential increase (for example, weights may no longer be considered as exerting only pressure but also as having position, etc.).

2. Secondly, the success of compensating regulations leads to greater discrimination (or differentiation). As a result, elements that couldn't be assimilated at first become constituents of a new subscheme or subcategory. Naturally this discrimination is in itself an enrichment, but in addition, as a necessary complement, it calls for an integration proportional to the discrimination. Furthermore, any discrimination constitutes a new kind of possible disturbance in relation to the cohesion of the whole system; either the whole

system is then interrupted or else this cohesion (preserving interactions) exercises its assimilating power on the differentiated subsystems, the differentiation is compensated for by an integration, and a new enrichment due to the equilibration is acquired.

It should be well understood that this integrating power of totalities is not a *deus ex machina* arising for an occasion without the fresh work of a differentiation; it is the result of the characteristics of assimilation (if one talks of a *deus*, it is then the *deus* of life in general in all its manifestations and not only of the cognitive functions).

Any process of assimilation is necessarily cyclic and self-preserving, hence the resistance of a total system (of any rank) to differentiations and compensating reactions in the form of integrations. Here let us recall that all the cognitive regulations are due to the assimilation-accommodation bi-polarity which is common to schemes and to all systems as well as to their cyclic characteristic—this characteristic itself forms a necessary condition of the assimilation.[13] The equilibrium seen as mutual conservation, differentiations, and integrations is therefore merely a special case of ac-

---

[13] It is essential to emphasize the differences between the compensations in cycles characterizing the behavior schemes (as well as the biological organizations), and those which intervene in a physical equilibrium or in a "moderation" in the sense of the Le Chatelier-Braun principle. For example, when on a scale the action of the weights compensate each other, and the arm merely serves as mediator transmitting these opposite actions. Or when a piston in a container compresses a gas which becomes hot and tends to dilate, and in so doing moderates the piston's action, the walls of the container merely serve as a passive mediator, etc. In an assimilation scheme, $(A \times A') \rightarrow (B \times B') \rightarrow \ldots \rightarrow (A \times A')$, the links between each pair form a source of action in the sense that the cycle as such tends to conserve itself. The actions and reactions between A and A', if we modify A' into A'', thus concern these two elements only (as though they were opposite weights on a scale) but are bound up with the entire cycle. The resistance of A to the modification of A' into A'' thus depends not only on A but on all the other elements, B, C, etc., and the active connections linking each pair to each of the others (see §1). It is this relative stability of the whole as cycle or system

commodations (or elementary compensations) and assimilations.

3. We now must consider an essential problem. Each assimilation scheme includes a certain accommodation capacity, i.e., it has certain limits beyond which the cycle forming the scheme would rupture. We could speak of an "accommodation standard" in the same sense as in biology we have a "reaction standard" for all phenotypes possible for a certain genotype. This accommodation standard naturally depends on the joint resistance and plasticity of the cycle producing the assimilation, but in the present state of knowledge we can only judge a condition when we see observable results, and we are unable to furnish laws or a detailed model. A second factor is more accessible: this is the number of elementary schemes or subsystems (connected schemes) already constructed in the total system. The higher this number becomes, the greater is the accommodation standard of the scheme considered[14] since probabilities for connections increase; and if this is the case, the number of regulations also increases with the number of possible accommodations. But the contrary is also true, that is, the greater the accommodation standard of an elementary scheme (we could also call it "assimilation standard"), the greater are the chances of the scheme entering into reciprocal assimilation relations with others and thus of forming new subsystems within the whole.

The third category of enrichments, due to the regulations and equilibrations, which includes both the increase in the accommodation standards and the facilitation of the formation of new subsystems with new connections and necessary

---

which plays the chief role in the new accommodations or compensations. The force of cohesion due to cyclic links intervenes as an endogenous factor when the exogenous modification of A' into A'' transforms A into A_2 without destroying the cohesion of the scheme thus modified at this or that point.

[14] Cf. Zipf's law in the model given by Mandelbrot, one of the consequences of which is that the number of species increases with that of the types.

"relativisations" (in our research on contradiction, we have seen that excess is not only due to the extension of the referential but also, and this in "comprehension," to the "relativisation" of the predicates initially considered in absolute forms).

4. Let us now turn to the improvements inherent in increasing equilibration which are no longer simply the result of the success of regulation but are derived from the very structure of these regulations. The most general progress is attributable to the gradual construction of the negations of various orders. This doubtless is the most important enrichment, for we have seen (§2) that these constructions form a necessary condition of the equilibrium and that their initial deficiency, as compared to the systematic primacy of the affirmations, constitutes the cause for the nonbalance (§3) which occurs so frequently, is profound and difficult to surmount, and characteristic of the preoperational stages (e.g.), lack of conservation, etc.).

The compensating regulations are not expressed directly in the subject's awareness, and the observations at play are at first conceived only in terms of differences. But the practical and in a way driving negations are nevertheless of great importance, for they are at the source of eventual conceptualized negations. The analysis, purely descriptive, that we have given in §2 of the role of negations in an equilibration can be inserted, on a trial basis, in a psychogenetic explanation. The conceptualization of schemes, for example, into a classification such as $A + A' = B$; $B + B' = C$, etc.,[15] actually supposes as many negations as there are positive elements because $A' = B \cdot (non\text{-}A)$ and $A = B \cdot (non\text{-}A')$, etc. Moreover, the whole set of opposite operations which develop at the operational stages is the outcome of these conceptualizations which are founded on the negations in the action required by the compensating regulations at the inception of their sensorimotor forms. It is the equili-

---

[15] This has no relation to the symbolism of the cycles discussed in §1 and taken up again in §2.

bration functioning as compensation between the affirmations and the negations which is thus directed by the very structure of the regulations.

5. The reflection of functional negations in conceptual negations is an expression of a construction process and the regulations. The mechanism of the "reflecting abstraction,"[16] interferes with the formation of the regulations of regulations and this occurs to such a degree that there seems to be a single mechanism analyzed in two languages and from two different viewpoints.

The "reflecting abstraction" includes two inseparable aspects: a "reflecting" in the sense of projecting on an upper level what is happening on a lower level, and a "reflection" in the sense of a cognitive reconstruction or reorganization (more or less conscious) of what has thus been transferred. It should be mentioned that this abstraction is not limited to using a series of hierarchic levels whose formation would be foreign to it: it is the abstraction that produces them by alternate interactions of "reflecting" and "reflection," in such close connection with the refinement of the regulations that a single method unit is operative.

a. First, let us recall that any regulation works both in a "retroactive" manner and on anticipation (hence the variations of amplitude of the corrections and the reinforcements). Anticipations are based on cues (the newborn picks up signals very early and can recognize feeding time during the first week), and the cues coordinate according to a law known as "transference" or better still as "recurrence": a announces x, then b preceding a announces a and x, then c preceding b announces b, a, and x, etc. It is then clear that this organization of cues constitutes a new level—the initial regulations proceed merely by corrections and reinforcements. In the evolution of serializations, from the level of pairs or trios to systematic operational serializations, a level of success exists where the corrections gradually coordinate, due to anticipatory and "retroactive" progress, become in-

---

[16] A review of the work on abstraction is to be published.

creasingly rare, and finally useless. This means an intermediary representative level is formed between the simple action of physical groping and the programmed operation. Thus we see in the elaboration of the "reflecting" process the role of regulations on a level produced by their very coordinations.

b. Each new level gives rise, in the form we called "reflection," to new equilibrations by regulation (clues, etc.), and these regulations of somewhat superior rank naturally extend those of the initial level by "reflective abstraction."

c. Obviously, the reciprocal also is valid: the superior system constitutes a regulator controlling the regulations of the lower level. This is true at all levels where a "reflection" intervenes, as the "reflection" constitutes an adjustment by its very nature "on" the previously acquired knowledge. Thus the "reflection" represents the prototype of a regulation of regulations, since by itself it is a regulator and regulates what is insufficiently regulated by previous regulations. This is apparent when we study active adjustments or when the conceptualization directs action; but this mechanism is renewed at every stage,[17] the inclusion of a new "reflection" being what characterizes the formation of any new stage of development.

d. This formation of the regulations of regulations, whether we express it in this language or in that of reflections or of reflections characteristic of the reflective ab-

---

[17] For example, in experiments on the conservation of matter a small ball is modified into blood sausage (see §19). The discovery (by progressive regulation of observation at first poorly recorded) of a nonplanned thinning out of this sausage is extended in anticipation of variations in length and diameter. But this anticipation produces a new level of "reflection" which then allows a "reflection" on the transformations as such in opposition to the original states and conclusions; hence, there is comprehension of the responsible characteristic for these variations—in (+) and (−) and finally conservation. Such methods of regulation and "reflection" combined produce the regulations we just discussed.

straction, thus constitutes a very general and apparently paradoxical process according to which any cognitive system is dependent on the following one for control and the completion of its regulation. It is in this manner (corresponding moreover to many examples in contemporary mathematics[18]) that a self-regulation is gradually developed, that is, by a play of differentiations and integrations as is shown by totalities acting as regulators on the subsystems and the special schemes in the sense described in §4 (see also §3).

6. This collaboration of regulations and reflective abstraction, both evolving from level to level, takes into account the central process of the cognitive development, that is, the undefined formation of operations on operations. In fact, regulations of regulations exist, and if, as we have shown elsewhere,[19] reflections of various powers also exist, it is obvious that on a given operational system it will always be possible to apply new operations taken from other systems; those most frequently taken will be from the preceding schemes in the very heart of the same system which have been raised to a superior power (like the additions of additions, the source of numerical multiplications).

These constructions are inseparable from compensations in the sense that the additions aim to fill a gap, the source of nonbalance. For example, the "constituting functions," which form at about the age of five, are one-way applications (unequivocally "on the right") and they must be completed in the other direction, hence the operational reversibility at the seven- or eight-year-old level.

7. If the constructions described in sections 3 and 4 are taken from the very structure of regulations, and not only from the results of successful compensations, the principle of creative novelties, as expressed by the cognitive development of this general regulating structure (which constitutes the most important example of increasing equilibra-

---

[18] See in the *Etude* on *La généralisation* (to be published).
[19] See *L'abstraction* (*Etude* to be published).

tion), explains the very formation of operations. In fact, the operations, insofar as they always appear as pairs of direct and opposite (or reciprocal) operations, constitute the final point of improvement of the regulations and thus represent "perfect" regulations (according to the Ashby term) as much by the generalization of "retroactions" as by the exact compensation of affirmations and negations. (We will return to this in §13.)

§7/ *Conclusion*

In summary, if the cognitive equilibration, in the majority of situations, is a progression toward a better equilibrium, it is then impossible to distinguish what in these increasing equilibrations is due to compensations, that is, the equilibration as such, and what offers constructions proper. Constructions are indicated by new compositions or the extension of the field, and in principle are capable of proceeding from the subject's spontaneous initiatives (inventions, etc.) and from chance encounters with the objects in the environment (discoveries, etc.). In fact, these two aspects of development are complementary and bound up with each other for two reasons. On the one hand, any new construction calls for compensations because it inserts itself in re-equilibration processes (to correct certain defects or previous limitations or to modify the process of differentiations and integrations[20]) along with its own regulations. On the other hand, any increasing equilibration involves the necessity of new constructions and vice-versa, as we have just seen in §6.

It is worth noting that such a proposition does not simply

---

[20] See our discussion of the mechanism of "constructive generalizations" which in their "synthesizing" as well as "complementing" forms are always compensating while also being constructive. (A study on generalizing, with new information on equilibration of differentiations and integrations, is in preparation.)

result from a theoretical analysis of basic notions (in particular from analysis of the relations between the assimilation and the accommodation) imposed on us by our previous work on cognitive development. Recently it has received an experimental confirmation with the fine research on learning by Inhelder. Sinclair, and Bovet.[21] In a study of the relations between learning and development, these authors showed that the most fruitful factors in the acquisition of understanding were the results of disturbances producing conflicting situations (for example, conflicts between ordering lengths using ordinal numbers and giving these lengths cardinal numbers for measurement, etc.) which once handled in a systematic manner involve the excesses and new constructions. Of special interest is the fact that a device was found to create conflicts only on certain given levels for the structure in question. In other words, a device is not a disturber in itself, but, on the contrary, is conceived as a disturbance or is not one according to the elements that have been acquired by the structure in formation. Such facts are highly significant for an understanding of the close union of constructions and compensations.

To return to theoretical notions, it seems clear that at the very outset of the activity processed by the elementary action schemes this union reveals itself each time a scheme is summoned to proceed to an accommodation and consequently to a renewed assimilation. In fact, the object not yet assimilated and not immediately capable of being assimilated constitutes an obstacle (capable either of remaining minor or increasing) and a new accommodation is then necessary. But as the assimilation and the accommodation constitute two poles, and not two distinct behaviors, it is clear that the new assimilation plays the construction role (extension of the scheme field, introduction of new articulations in the cycle, etc.) and the new accommodation that of compensation (new adjustments in reciprocity or inversion of the object's unforeseen characteristics). Each of

21 *Loc. cit.*, 1974.

these two orientations is bound up with the other in an indivisible whole.

In general, if we recall that the cognitive systems actually function through three kinds of equilibrium—those between the assimilation of schemes of action and the accommodation of these to the objects, those between the schemes or subschemes of the same rank, and those between the partial systems with their differentiations and the total scheme with its integration—it follows that with any action or operation, including a teleonomy, the new means to be used should involve the first two kinds of equilibration and the new goals the last. Thus both goals and means subject the new constructions to the requirements of the compensations. Reciprocally, the essential driving forces of the cognitive development being the external nonbalance (from application difficulties and the effects of the operations on the objects) and internal nonbalance (difficulties of composition) as well as the reequilibrations which this nonbalance involves, sooner or later the equilibration will be increasing and constitute a going-beyond process as much as a stabilization, thus uniting the constructions and the compensations within the functional cycles.

This intimate union of constructions and compensations, characterizing the increasing equilibration of the cognitive systems, actually seems linked to the cycle characteristic shown by these systems which distinguishes them (in common with the biological cycles) from the physical systems in equilibrium. As we have already said, in physical equilibrium the elements are both independent and antagonistic. On the contrary, in an operational system we find the remarkable situation in which an inverse operation, T^{-1}, is oriented in a direction opposite to that of the direction operation, T, and yet produced or, so to speak, called into existence by the sole fact of the possibility of T. Here, let us recall, is a general characteristic of the cognitive equilibrations: even in a sensorimotor scheme, the assimilation and the accommodation, although from a certain viewpoint opposed to each other, necessarily involve each other, so that the conflict situation between the subject's action and the resistance of objects is immediately accentuated. The resistance of objects resembles the antagonisms characteristic of the balances of physical forces. Reciprocal assimilation and accommodation between schemes and subsystems of the same rank are first relatively opposed as distinct and independent, but the equilibration of their coordinations makes them mutually responsible while conserving their distinct sources of negation (if $B = A + A'$ then A' is complementary to A, hence the negation of A under B). In the equilibrium between the differentiation and the integration, the situation is even more paradoxical, since the differentiation threatens the conservation of the integration while at the same time reinforcing it. Generally speaking, we can thus say that not only do the opposed mechanisms attract each other like opposite charges of electricity, but they also produce each other, which implies a closed cycle capable of increasing and enriching itself while conserving its cyclic form (cf. §1). This explains the fact that the constructions and compensations are inseparable, for if the whole is to conserve the parts, and vice versa, during each modification, there must be simultaneous production and conservation.

Two

THE FUNCTIONING
OF THE EQUILIBRATION
AND THE STAGES
OF THE COMPENSATION

We have attempted to supply an explanatory scheme for equilibration and will now study how this develops concretely during interactions between the subject and the objects. In those concrete situations which we studied in detail (see *La prise de conscience* and *Réussir et comprendre*), we were first of all confronted with the question of how equilibration of observations on the action and on the object works if it distinguishes the characteristics of the object which belong to it in its content (hence, the empirical abstraction) and also those (order, relationships, etc.) which are introduced there as forms by a subject's coordinated actions. Next we studied the nature of the equilibrium of the inferential coordinations constructed by the subject on his own actions and the coordinations attributed to objects during attempts at casual explanation, etc. It is especially worthwhile to perceive the cycle form (or spiral, insomuch as the cycle is not completed) which will be developed by the equilibration of observations and coordinations.

We can then return to the problem of disturbances and compensations and, instead of continuing to insist on their common characteristic as in §5, consider the very different stages they present during an increasing equilibration; their changes during internalization vary, to an important degree, their role in the cognitive systems. When the disturbances arise in the form of outside accidents, compensations are to cancel or neutralize them; both finally are integrated in the operational systems, the disturbances as foreseeable variations deducible from the objects, and the compensations as contrary operations.

If we study the general process of internalization (see §13), we will see that the equilibration necessarily includes exact compensation of the negations and affirmations. However, the initial nonbalance is due to a consistent primacy of the positive elements—the negations at that stage cannot be constructed by the subject and are limited to those which, so to speak, are imposed from without.

§8/ The Observables and the Coordinations

Let us begin with a few definitions and remarks.

1. An "observable" is that which experience makes it possible to identify by an immediate reading of the given events themselves, whereas a "coordination" includes inferences and thus involves more than the observables. However, such a distinction is clear only on levels where the subject is capable of objective observation and of logically valid inferences, whereas their delimitation is less marked when the identifications are in fact inexact and the inferences include false assumptions. It is insufficient, therefore, to define the observable merely by its perceived characteristics, since the subject often believes that he perceives what actually he does not perceive and characterizes the coordinations by verbal formulation, adequate or riddled with

errors. It is evident that the implicit inferences play a role as great, if not greater, than the partial perceptions. The observables must therefore be defined by what the subject believes he perceives and not simply by what is perceivable.

2. In other words, an identification is never independent of the recording instruments (hence of an assimilation) available to the subject, and these instruments are never solely perceptive but are influenced by preoperational or operational schemes capable of modifying or distorting the perceived entity. But as these schemes are, moreover, those used by the coordinations, the observables themselves are most often conditioned by previous coordinations. If, therefore, we consider an observable with coordinations at level N, we must remember that such observables do not constitute first facts but themselves ordinarily depend on observables and coordinations from the level $N - 1$, and so forth. Even at the elementary levels, apparent close to the birth of the subject, observables are part of a network of coordinations, but these are partly innate (involving reflexes, etc.) and are not only progressively inferred.

3. It should also be noted that we distinguish between the observables verified by the subject through his own actions and the observables recorded on the object. For example, when a small ball of clay is transformed into a sausage, one observable intervenes relative to the action, which concerns the act of stretching, and at least one observable relative to the object, that is, its extension. Here again, it is difficult to establish the dividing lines, but since one of the essential factors of the equilibration characteristic of level N is precisely the springing up of second observables (object) on the first (action), the question of delimitations is less important than the interactions of the subject and the object.

4. The coordinations are characterized by the inferences, implicit or explicit, which the subject considers or uses as if they imposed themselves on him, with all the indeterminate possibilities between subjective evidence and logical necessity. These necessary or pseudonecessary inferences are not

simply the result of inductive generalizations, hence the extension of a few verifications of observable relations to "all," but rather are constructions of new relations which go beyond the boundaries of the observable. For example, the anticipation that a shock from a ball A against a ball B will always be followed by movement by B will not be called "coordination," whereas this term will be applied to a proposition such as "the élan of A has passed to B," since a transmission of movement is never observable in itself.

5. However, since the observables are often poorly observed (see this section, paragraphs 2 and 3), would it not be essential to call necessary inference or coordination any error dealing with the observables? Here it is worthwhile to distinguish two kinds of errors. The first is the erroneous observation which results from a coordination which is itself false and yet well delimited; for example, the idea that any mediate transmission implies a slight translation of the mediators to bring the child aged seven to ten to "see" immobile mediators "move." In this case, it is easy to distinguish the false verification of the illusory coordination when even the first results from the second. The second kind of error involves a false verification inspired not by a well-determined inferential coordination but by gaps or overly inconclusive coordinations. For example, a water level can be "observed" as not horizontal because it is conceived as depending only on the form of the jar and as not bearing any relation to outside references. In this case, the observable is not directly deduced from the coordinations in play but is relatively independent, and the distinction between what is the observable and its general context remains a fortiori easy.

6. Finally it is worth distinguishing the coordinations between the actions, which are preoperational, or the subject's operations, and the coordinations between the objects insofar as they are supposed to act on one another. The coordinations between the objects involve operations attributed to the objects, hence a causal model. An example of the

first type of coordinations is that of the transitivity of relations established by the subject. An example of the second is the transmission of movement between objects, which is also a kind of transitivity but attributed to the powers of the objects themselves.

7. There is a third type of coordination which deals with the object's momentary characteristics but has them introduced by the subject; for example, the equivalence between two rows of coins which the subject arranges end to end. In this situation, it is evident that the coordination is between the subject's actions or operations and not between objects, although the results are read from the objects, i.e., the operations in play are applied to them ("pseudoempirical" abstraction). Let us consider: (a) The action (for example, pushing) which deals with the objects does not modify them by using their previous characteristics, but it adds new characteristics which remain momentary—order, perceptible relations, sum in each row, etc. (b) The reading of this operational limit imposed on the objects merely deals with its extratemporal aspect neglecting, in conformity with the subject's intentions, the durations, speeds, and dynamic quality of the acts present in these arrangements. (c) Each reading neglects a fortiori the kinematic and dynamic characteristics of the objects (resistance, weight, etc.). (d) The coordinations in play in these situations are therefore of a logico-mathematical nature (coordinations between the orders, between the sums, etc.) and disregard causal coordinations. (e) The coordinations between the observables verified on the objects are identical to those of the actions and not only analogous of approximatively isomorphic, as is the case between causal and logico-mathematical coordinations. (f) In fact, the operations in play are merely applied and not attributed to the objects, since the objects are not part of a correspondence but serve merely as points of application for the subject's operations.

§9/   The Elementary Interactions, Type I

The general model of interaction which we will use to pose the problem of the equilibration from the functional viewpoint, and which we will call type II, will show how the observables recorded on the action are subordinated to those which are dependent on the object, and hence yield a better conceptualized coordination of the subject's actions. The problem then is to understand how the observables of action and those of the supporting object are related; it is this elementary interaction that we would like to designate as type I. We will first analyze this elementary interaction, with the understanding that it will appear as part of the whole process (type II).

1. Among the interactions of type I, we must distinquish two varieties to mark the differences in function between the causal and logico-mathematical actions. Disregarding kinematic or dynamic components, a subject's action can be considered in its material, or physical, aspects, and insofar as it modifies the objects with which it deals it can change them only by enriching them with timeless forms (order, meetings, etc.). Therefore, the interactions of type I are relative only to the observables (with the inferential coordinations yet to occur), and we can distinguish the following two cases: type IA in which the observations in play intervene within a causal action, and type IB in which the observables are subject to a logico-mathematical action.

2. Let us consider an example of type IA using the most precociously assimilated causal situation—that in which the subject pushes an object. Let us call Ms the subject's movement in the direction of the object or in the direction imprinted on the object. Let us call Ps the thrust exerted by the subject on the object. Let us remember also that this thrust can be stronger or weaker and that the regulation of this force is inseparable from that of the movement Ms. The "feeling of effort" here consists in a simple observation of what Janet called the "effort behavior" and which he char-

acterized as an acceleration regulation. The effort thus concerns both *Ps* and *Ms*.

3. Let us now distinguish the two observables concerning the object and corresponding to *Ps* and *Ms*: the resistance of the object, *Ro*, which can be strong, weak, or almost nil as compared to *Ps*; and the movement of the object, or *Mo*, which depends both on its resistance and the subject's action.

4. Now if we stick to the functional dependencies, in other words, to the orientated but observable covariations, with as yet no causal inference or coordination going beyond the observable, we obtain the following two functions which the subject becomes aware of and conceptualizes: (*a*) the complex *Ms* → *Ps* which depends on the resistance, *Ro*, of the object, since the subject's effort is measured as a function of this perceived resistance; (b) reciprocally, the movement of the object, *Mo*, which is a function of this complex, *Ms* → *Ps*, since this movement is verified according to the subject's action.

5. Thus we have the elementary interaction of type IA:

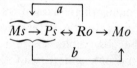

Let us recall that, contrary to the interactions of type II where, in addition to observables, inferential coordinations will intervene, here we will only consider observables relative either to the subject's action (*Ms* and *Ps*) or to the object (*Ro* and *Mo*). As for the two functions *a* and *b*, working in opposite directions, these are verifiable and related covariations which are direct and perceptively controllable.[1] We will thus speak of *a* and *b* as relations be-

---

[1] These covariations, orientated and expressing dependencies, are thus functions, and the interaction IA (as well as IB) therefore constitutes an elementary form of "category" in the sense understood by McLane and Eilenberg—let us use the term "precategory." We

tween observables (or interactions of type I), themselves observable and opposed to the inferential coordinations intervening in the interactions of type II. Certainly if the subject is to attain the observables *a* and *b*, and even *Ms*, *Ps*, *Ro*, and *Mo*, he requires recording instruments in the form of preoperations or often operations proper (categories, relations, functions, identities, etc.), but these serve merely as logico-mathematical intermediaries which read physical facts (of the action or of the subject) and not as inferential instruments as they intervene in the coordinations of type II.

6. But to establish the ideas, let us give an example of the inferential coordinations in play in type II. We can investigate those which the subject can take, and take unfailingly, from the interactions of type IA (analyzed in section 5). From the action, $Ms \rightarrow Ps$, regulated on the object, *Ro*, and from the movement acquired by the object, *Mo*, which depends reciprocally on the action $Ms \rightarrow Ps$, the subject will infer (either by a representative inference or even in certain cases by a preinference based on the perceptive or driving regulations) that something has been transmitted between the subject's action and the object. Now, this transmission is not observable as such. Even in purely perceptual situations, we neither "see" nor "feel" anything pass from the agent to the subject; hence, we will limit ourselves here to speaking of perceiving an overall result. Thus in this situation an inferential (or preinferential) mechanism intervenes, that is, a coordination peculiar to type II, expressed both in terms of a "production" (change of state of the object) and of at least partial conservation (*Mo* coming from *Ms*).

7. Before going on to type IB, let us note that the interaction IA (see section 5) is specific to situations involving the subject's action. If we consider only two objects, *A* (active) and *B* (passive), we rediscover the observables *MA*, *PA*, *RB*, and *MB*, but unless the experimenter varies

must emphasize that we are dealing with functions and not implications; the arrows merely indicate the directions the functions take.

MA and *PA* as a function of a resistance, *RB*, known in advance, the function *a* does not intervene. In Michotte's visual perceptive causality, the observable *RB* (which moreover Michotte neglects) is known merely as a function of *MB*. That is why we believe that the visual perceptive causality implies the tactile-kinesthetic causality—that it is limited to transposing or expression in visual terms when the subject does not touch the objects.

8. Let us now study the interactions of type IB which link the observables in the actions of logico-mathematical forms. We distinguish the following four observables: *As* which expresses the subject's activity or operation (seriation, classification, etc.); *Fs* which is the application of the operation, hence the form imposed by the subject on the objects (connection of relations, categories, etc.); *Ro* which is the resistance, actual or not, presented by the objects to this being placed in a form (the submission or refusal of the objects to being manipulated); and *Mo* which is the modification of the collection of objects, enriched (owing to $As \rightarrow Fs$) by a new form. Thus we have

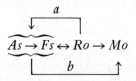

The great difference between the IB and IA types of interaction is that in IA the observables *Ms* and *Ps* correspond to the subject's outlays (outlays of effort, hence of movement and thrust) and a gain of movement, *Mo*, for the object. In IB, on the contrary, the form *Fs*, which the subject applies to the objects, is not lost for this subject and therefore does not mean for him an outlay but the production of a morphism which enriches his knowledge. As for the activity outlay, *As*, it plays no role in *Mo* insofar as the logico-mathematical forms dismiss the dynamic and kinematic quality of the interaction.

Moreover, the resistance of objects, Ro, constitutes in IA a force (reaction) oriented in a direction opposite to the action, whereas in IB only acceptance is at issue (correspondence between form and content)—if a partial or total refusal relative to the planned operation or incompatibility occurs, the subject uses other operations. However, we will see in §22 and §23 to what degree form and content are in fact complex when the first does not limit itself to retaining certain aspects of the second but momentarily brushes them aside without knowing it.

9. As for the inferential coordinations (interactions of type II) arising from interactions of type IB, these are then simply "applied" to the objects and not "attributed" as in IA, where causal actions, for example, the inferred transmission (see section 6), are no longer seen as the subject's operation but as a physical process inherent in the objects (hand or passive moving object)—conceived as themselves being the operators. Consequently, in these interactions, IB or IIB, the observables related to the actions or operations (As, Fs, etc.) are again found on the objects (Mo) in identical forms, at least up to and including the stage of operations known as "concrete," since they are made only by means of actions exerted on these objects. It is obvious, on the other hand, that on the level of hypothetical deductive operations the material objects cannot intervene and be replaced by mere symbols. It is also obvious that if, up to and including the level of concrete operations, the subject's activity, As, should often be distinguished from the application of the forms imposed on the objects, Fs, this distinction loses all meaning at the stage of formal operations, since the activity, As, is then reduced to a purely mental construction of these forms.

Finally it should be noted that if (as we have seen in §8) the observables always depend on previous coordinations (preoperational or causal), there will be a notable difference between the interactions IA (or IIA) and IB (or IIB). In the IA and IIA interactions a combination of empirical abstractions (from objects), and reflective abstractions (from coordinations of the subject's actions) will intervene, whereas in IB and IIB only the latter and "pseudoempirical abstractions" will be in play, since the Mo characteristics result solely from the projection of Fs forms, which are themselves taken from the subject's previous coordinations (preoperational or purely operational).

On the whole, the interactions of type I express the simplest form of equilibration (symbolized above by the double arrow $\leftrightarrow$): that which is established between the assimilation, indicated by a scheme ($Ms + Ps$ or $As + Fs$), and the accommodation to the objects ($Ro + Mo$).

§ *10/   The Interactions of Type* IIA

In type II interactions both the observables of type I (A and B) and inferential coordinations intervene. In what follows we will thus unite the observables Ms and Ps (or Ms and Fs), etc., under the overall term of $Obs.$ S, or "observables relative to the subject's action," and the observables Ro and Mo, etc., under the designation $Obs.$ O or "observables relative to the objects." We will also use the abbreviations $Coord.$ $S.$, to denote "the subject's inferential coordinations of actions (or operations)," and $Coord.$ O, to denote "inferential coordinations between objects." Both are kinematic and dynamic, hence causal, for operations attributed to these objects in IIA situations, although they are only operational in IIB, or for simply applied coordinations.

1. If we consider a single state of type IIA and not a series of levels with increasing equilibration, we can begin with the following general form (where the sign marks an overall, durable or momentary equilibrium)

$$
\begin{array}{c}
OS \\[-2pt]
\downarrow \overline{\hspace{8em}} \rceil \\[-2pt]
(Obs.\ S \rightarrow Coord.\ S) \leftrightarrow (Obs.\ O \leftarrow Coord.\ O). \\[-2pt]
\lfloor \underline{\hspace{8em}} \uparrow \\[-2pt]
SO
\end{array}
$$

The two processes in play, *OS* and *SO*, with their regulations and local equilibrations concern the observables and the coordinations, and thus show none of the relative symmetry of functions *a* and *b* in type I interactions. Yet they express (in cycle form) the fundamental interaction of the subject and objects within any cognitive step; on the one hand, the subject achieves a clear knowledge of his own actions only from their effects on the objects, and on the other hand, he succeeds in understanding the latter only by inference from the coordinations of these same actions.

2. Thus the significance of the process *OS* is essentially related to the awareness (in its insufficiencies or its adequacies) of the action itself. We should not represent awareness as if it were a lightning illumination at a given moment of what the adaptations and driving regulations have accomplished during the success or failure of the preceding acts. The process is more complex:[2] the awareness of a physical action consists of its internalization in the form of representations, and the latter by no means lend themselves to simple mental images, copying the active procedures, but include a conceptualization due to the necessity of reconstructing on a consciousness level what has been achieved on a physical level. Thus it is normal that the observables relative to the action (*Obs. S*) remain not only incomplete but also are often erroneous and sometimes even systematically distorted insofar as they are placed in a precise relationship with the observables relative to the objects (*Obs. O*), since the observables indicate the results of the action and the awareness begins at the periphery to rise to the mechanism for production, and is therefore not centrifugal.

3. Thus this process *OS* includes an interaction of type I in its casual (IA) or operational (IB) forms or in the two combined (this is especially evident with spatial structurations, as the subject's space is operational and the object's space is always linked to a dynamic quality). We can think

[2] See our earlier studies *La prise de conscience* and *Réussir et comprendre*.

of process *OS* as working in two directions: in the direction leading from *Obs. O* to *Obs. S* (as function *a* in interaction I) and in the opposite direction from *S* to *O* (as function *b* in interaction I). It is worth recalling, however, that interaction I, by definition dealing only with the observables, results from an artificial cutting-out method and always continues, in behavior, in inferential coordinations (as we have seen in section 6 and §9). In reality, the comparison of observables *Obs. S* and *Obs. O* (hence functions *a* and *b* of interaction I) therefore creates inferential coordinations *Coord. S*, and interaction I describes the relation between the action observables and those of the object which prepare these *Coord. S*; these observables include in addition necessary inferences (subjective or objective).

Generally, the process *OS* therefore has the dominant direction leading from *Obs. O* to the *Obs. S*, since it is the *Obs. S*, once illuminated by *Obs. O*, which makes the formation of the *Coord. S* possible. Naturally this dominant direction does not exclude many regulations; hence we have the intervention of local retroactions of the form

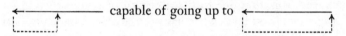

But since the process linking the *Coord. S* to the *Coord. O* necessarily includes activity in the direction *SO*, for reasons we are about to discuss, it is clear that the process *OS* necessarily presents the reciprocal dominant direction *Obs. O → Obs. S*.

4. The process *SO*, leading from coordinations of the action, *Coord. S*, to those of the object, *Coord. O*, actually expresses the fundamental fact that to understand, or even to discover, the causal relations between the objects, the subject has to pass through the intermediary of his own operations. The reason for this is obvious: since the causal relations overreach the boundaries of the observable, any dynamic coordination between the objects implies the use of necessary inferences (in opposition to the inducible gen-

eralizations) or simply extensions which are "legal" but are not necessary, as they know no control other than a logically insufficient verification made from observables.[3] If these inferences are necessary, they can only be operational or preoperational, that is, based on the general coordinations of the action (order, interlocking, correspondences, transitivity, etc.); and this endogenous source of the process SO, which imposes itself in interactions of form IIA, will be found also a fortiori in forms of IIB but again, naturally, with local feedback possibilities of the type described in section 3, which result from "return" actions of the contents on the forms. Everything that we have found from our extensive research on causality shows these inevitable pathways of the subject's operational compositions (hence, the *Coord. S*) required to reach the coordinations between objects, and these are possible insofar as the coordinations extend beyond the boundaries of the observables. Let us recall that isolated operations intervene the moment these observables are read but that they depend on inferences, and thus the fact that they extend beyond the observable implies also recourse to the compositions *Coord. S*.

5. The basic facts lead us to consider the interactions of type II as constituents of a sequential process of equilibration dealing with a number of successive states, n, and therefore extending beyond the form of a single state as described in section 1.

The first of these facts is that, as we have already indicated in §8, an observable generally depends, directly or indirectly, on previous coordinations with their success or insufficiencies. This is especially true when erroneous verifications are dictated by false presuppositions. It is therefore evident that the state described in section 1 depends on previous states, including the *Obs. S* and *Obs. O*.

It is evident that, reciprocally, the coordinations de-

---

[3] The exception would be Popper's "falsifiability," which subordinates them also to inferences extending beyond the observable.

scribed in this state (*Coord. S* and *Coord. O*) create, sooner or later, the discovery of observables in order to gain better verification or begin research for verification. For example, in experiments on observations of a ball's impact on the side of another (not involving a direct hit), when the subject begins to understand why the ball is unable to continue in the direction of the first movement, he better observes directions as well as the exact locations of impact points, etc. It is therefore clear that, until the usually tardy access to sufficiently precise models is achieved, we witness a series of states showing progressive equilibration, with initial stages reaching only unstable forms of equilibrium because of their gaps, disturbances, and above all because of actual or virtual contradictions.

6. Thus the general model should take the following form:

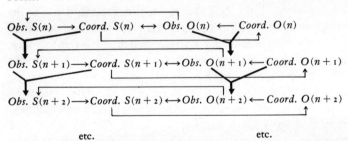

etc.   etc.

Each *Obs. S* of a given row is thus a function (thick, oblique lines) of the *Obs. S* and *Coord. S* of the preceding row, and each *Obs. O* is likewise a function of the *Obs. O* and *Coord. O* of the previous level. Thus in like manner the *Obs.* of the initial row is a function of the more elementary levels.

7. It now is possible to fill the gaps already pointed out in the discussion of our initial model.[4] First, our new model can be applied to causality as much as to the subject's operations. Second, it deals with any number of observables and

[4] Vol. II of *Etudes, Logique et équilibre.*

coordinations. Third, each state includes its own form of equilibrium, stable or unstable, characterized on the one hand by the interactions between the subject on the level considered and the objects, certain characteristics of which are registered, and, on the other, by the relations between the observables and the coordinations. Fourth, in a special state, these relations or interactions involve, according to the situation, either sufficient coherence to stabilize the equilibrium or nonbalance—due to errors, gaps, or lack of intrinsic necessity—leading to a search for a better equilibrium. Furthermore, we at once see the possible role of contradictions between the observables themselves, when they are insufficiently conceptualized, or between these observables and the coordinations destined to link them by inferences dictated by necessity.

The difference between this new model and the preceding one is chiefly due to the formulation of relations between the empirical abstraction (from objects or observables) and the reflective abstraction (for coordinations of actions). In the earlier model the initial driving force consisted in probabilities of encounter with observable characteristics of the object, the reflecting abstraction only intervening later during operational coordinations or at the start of their operational rough outlines. In the present model, on the contrary, from the very outset there is interaction between the observables and the coordinations; hence there is collaboration on every level between the empirical and reflecting abstractions, the latter, as a result, continually playing the role of the required driving force.

Thus we see that, in spite of the constant emphasis in this chapter on causality and the action of the objects in all the elementary forms of knowledge, we by no means diminish (the contrary is true) the importance of the subject's activities—their intervention remains indispensable at every cognitive level.

8. In regard to the very functioning of the equilibration, it is worth noting that, since reading new observables pre-

cedes their coordination, the four mechanisms at work result in a cycle with the following order:

$$Obs.\ O \rightarrow Obs.\ S \rightarrow Coord.\ S \rightarrow Coord.\ O \rightarrow Obs.\ O \ldots$$

Three possibilities can then be envisioned.

a. There is rapid agreement between the conceptualized observations concerning the objects (*Obs. O*) and to the actions (*Obs. S*) as well as between the coordinations themselves and between the coordinations and the observables; in this event, the circle merely closes, that is, the final arrow (*Coord. O → Obs. O*) leads to no other modifications. A relatively stable equilibrium is thus reached as no new observations or reorganized inferences intervene (hence, the problem is momentarily solved).

b. Episodic contradictions and then local regulations occur between the *Obs. O* and *Obs. S*, and *Obs. S* and *Coord. S*, and *Coord. S* and *Coord. O* (or within the *Coord. S* or *Coord. O* if some of them use several structures and the compatibility between these utilizations is not immediate), and most importantly between the *Coord. O* (for example, in the causal explanation obtained from verifications and inferences) and the *Obs. O* (reinspection of the facts pertaining to the object). In this situation, there is short-term groping, then again relative equilibrium expressive of more or less durable stabilization.

c. The third possibility occurs if one or several of the various kinds of contradictions finally proves to be sufficiently resistant so that it cannot be removed by local readjustments; this situation is the result of actual or virtual conflicts between the coordinations and the observables—a conflict most frequent between *Coord. O* and *Obs. O* or between the coordinations themselves functioning as subsystems of variable extensions. The consequence is either the discovery of observables that until now had escaped notice during an all too summary investigation or a new conceptualization of previously recorded observables both of which lead to new coordinations; i.e., there is a nonbalance and a reequilibration which necessitates passing from a state n to a state $n + 1$, etc. (thick oblique lines in the model).

§11/ The Interactions of Type IIB and the Reflecting Abstraction

Just as the interactions of type IA correspond to those of type IB which deals solely with the subject's operations or preoperations, so too type IIA corresponds to type IIB which presents the same characteristics as IB but in addition involves the coordinations of the action or of the objects, in other words, the operational compositions made by the subject or applied to the objects. (The specific characteristic of such compositions is the ability to reach the inferences which logic requires.)

1. We will begin with situations in which the subject applies his preoperations or operations to material objects. This description will apply generally at the level of concrete operations, and can be seen at the twelve- to fifteen-year-old stage (for example, while making combinations, permutations, and arrangements), and even at different stages of scientific thought—depending on the difficulty of the problem to be solved. In studying problem solving, the question arises as to which method of progressive equilibration the subject uses to succeed in carrying out his operations on pure symbols which lead sooner or later to the formalization.

2. We again find a model identical in form to that of the preceding, but with the following modifications:

a. The observables on the action (*Obs. S*) here express the subject's awareness of operational intentions. Depending on the subject's stage of development, these intentions can remain vague and be modified during execution (preparatory stage) or, on the contrary, form a precise anticipatory scheme, in other words, already be dominated by the co-ordinations (*Coord. S*), hence by the previous operational compositions (including, for example, inferential transitivity for seriation of empirical seriations without transitivity being conceived as necessary).

b. The observables relative to the objects (*Obs. O*) consist in verifications made on the objects insofar as the objects have been modified, that is, grouped according to new criteria by the subject's action. This includes arrangement in orderly series, collections, categories, correspondences, etc. Thus there is the material realization of the subject's intentions (*Obs. S*).

c. The action coordinations (*Coord. S*) represent the preoperational or operational compositions which the subject projects and verifies, or which he discovers afterward, but in either case this occurs after comparison of *Obs. O* and *Obs. S*. Naturally these coordinations or compositions vary according to the subject's level of cognitive development.

d. The object coordinations (*Coord. O*) are then identical by complete isomorphism to those of the subject's operations (*Coord. S*) and not merely similar in attributions which then might suggest a causal relationship. In fact, the objects do not constitute operators independent of the subject but are coordinated insofar as they have characteristics (order, categories, etc.) conferred by this subject's very operations. Thus we see a simple (but precise) "application" of operational compositions to objects, in other words, of a "morphism" making it possible to read on the objects the subject's operational structures.

3. It is clear that passage from state n to state $n + 1$ cannot be due solely to contradictions at the preoperational levels. When the operational compositions are acquired, the system is more or less rapidly balanced in a stable manner, even if the subject requires reading *Obs. O* and coordinations between the objects (*Coord. O*) to dominate his own operations (*Coord. S*) as is the case at the level of "concrete" operations.

4. On reaching this level, progress leading from state n to $n + 1$ is then due to new requirements arising, for example,

from the resistance of the objects (see §9 for Ro in an interaction of type IB) appearing as a function in an unsolved problem, which forces the construction of new operations the moment the insufficiency of the preceding operational compositions is noticed. However, this new construction does not modify the previous operations and enriches them only by integrating them into a larger system. Thus new operations are constructed *on* preceding ones which serve as intermediaries (but there is no substitution) like arithmetical multiplication based on addition, or the "totality of the parts" (simplex). It is important to foresee the formation of "coordinations of coordinations" based on reflective activities in the system.

5. During these constructions of operations on operations, the role of objects (*Obs.* O) is gradually modified and increasingly important. Since they cannot change physically but merely be rearranged according to the various forms they assume, we must distinguish the following stages. At level n the *Obs.* O constitute the content of the first form which is applied to them, but at the $n + 1$ level it is this form which becomes the content for the form of the next superior type; however, the objects now merely constitute a content of content. At stage $n + 2$, it is the form $n + 1$ which, while already being a form of form, is found contained in the new one, whereas the objects lose their significance to an even greater degree. We then see why sooner or later it becomes easy for a subject to replace a concrete object with a symbolic object and to follow a path which will finally lead to formalizations.

6. In such situations the thick and oblique arrows of the present model correspond to purely reflective abstractions, whereas in the general model of §10, section 6, and in particular in casual systems, there is mingling of empirical abstractions (from observables) and reflecting abstractions (from operational coordinations). More precisely all that remains of the two pairs of sloping lines are the arrows on the right [*Coord.* $S(n)$ ⟋ *Obs.* $S(n + 1)$] and not those on the left [*Obs.* $S(n)$ ⟍ *Obs.* $S(n) + 1$)], unless the object's

observables are taken as indications of operational compositions. Furthermore—and it is all-important—since the subject's activities (*Obs. S*) blend more and more with the actual construction of new coordinations, the final model is reduced to a passage from coordinations of row n to those of row $n + 1$ with identity of coordinations of objects and actions or operations. This produces the level reached by the thinking process in "pure" mathematics.

7. The general model of §10, section 6, is that for the equilibration of knowledge in which a mingling of experimental observables and logico-mathematical structures, applied or attributed to the objects, intervened. The present model, on the contrary, is that for the equilibration of logico-mathematical knowledge only. Now if knowledge includes in its initial phases an experimental part (with abstraction from coordinations of actions but not of objects except for those dealing with momentary characteristics which the objects acquire under the effect of these coordinations), knowledge frees itself from this more or less rapidly. Nevertheless, among these logico-mathematical structures the simplest (categories and relation) present contents not determined by forms (for example, categories of objects formed according to the previously given qualities); however, the evolution of children from three to six (see §11) leads us to believe the construction of forms entirely determines their contents (which is seen to be the case with numbers); hence, we understand the purging which accompanies this progressive equilibration.

§*12/   The Interactions between Objects (Type IIC)*

The interactions studied thus far (IA and B, IIA and B) include all the subject's actions and, in the models which could be significant in causation (IA and IIA), it is these very actions which play the role of causes. As for the models IB and IIB, in these the subject's activities in themselves constitute operational "structurations." We will now study the situation in which objects act upon one another and in which the subject intervenes physically only by experiments whose sole aim is to dissociate the factors or to watch them vary as nature itself reaches the objects, with no more manipulation on the observer's part than that of astronomers regarding celestial movements.

1. In such situations, what until now we called the *Obs. S* or *Obs. O* will be replaced by observables dealing with the variations of presumed factors, i.e., either *Obs. X*—the *Obs O* will give way to observables related to the results noted on the dependent variables—or *Obs. Y* in the proposition where $Y = f(X)$ and where, naturally, this general expression will be able to cover several specific laws of forms $b = f(a)$, etc.

2. Nevertheless, the synthesis of these functional dependences or laws will lead to a structural model for logico-mathematical cognition necessarily constructed by means of the subject's operations. Consequently we can continue to use the term *Coord. S*. In addition, it is obvious that, insofar as this model can be "attributed" to the objects without being reduced to mere conventional language, it will be expressed in the form of a causal explanation which we will call *Coord. O*.

3. The interaction can be shown as follows:

$$(n) \quad (Obs.\ X \to Coord.\ S) \leftrightarrow (Obs.\ Y \to Coord.\ O)$$

with *YX* connecting over the top and *SO* connecting along the bottom.

The relationship of *YX* of the observed results, *Obs. Y*, to the variations of the factors, *Obs. X*, results therefore in the function $Y = f(X)$, whereas the relationship of the attributes of the model *Coord. S* to the coordination of the objects, *Coord. O*, expresses the causality. If this causal explanation remains in agreement with the observables *Y* and *X*, the system is in equilibrium. If not, the contradictions due to the facts or to their conceptualization induce revisions which achieve better balanced systems, $n + 1$, $n + 2$, as we have seen in the model illustrated in §10, section 6.

These remarks, however trivial, show (and this was their sole aim) that model IIA can be generalized to cover interactions between objects.

§13/   The Stages of the Compensation

We can now return to the problem of compensations (§5) to study the profound changes of functional significance which they show during increasing equilibrations and the evolution of regulations. Moreover, we will study the repercussions of these modifications on the internalization of negations and their construction by subject.

1. Mechanics defines equilibrium as the state in which the algebraic sum of the potential work compatible with the connections of the system considered is zero, in other words, as the state in which there is complete compensation of the possible changes.[5] It is obvious that in studying a cognitive system, if we ignore the underlying psychophysiological method and restrict ourselves to considering knowledge only, we do not deal with forces or with "work" (displacement of a force). On the other hand, if we speak merely of potential modifications in thinking either of outside facts impinging on the system but not yet considered by the subject, or of the actions or operations realizable but not yet made, the definition retains its full meaning; for either these modifications are sources of possible disturbances without compensating reactions—and the system, therefore, is not headed for equilibrium—or else the transformations, until then potential but planned and included in

---

[5] More precisely, the connections of the systems constitute the concrete realization of a "scheme of analogical calculation," producing compensations in case of nonbalance. The closing and requirements of the system are then based on the comprehension of "how the scheme calculates" and on the correlative organization of the extension.

the system (all the operations of a group, for example), are already compensated which tends to ensure the equilibrium of the whole.

However, if we define the equilibrium of the cognitive systems using the terms "virtual modifications" and their "compensations," we must note with care the different meanings "modifications" will acquire, whether they are disturbances or not, and use the term "compensations" so it takes into account the procedures they involve. We must distinguish three kinds of rather different behaviors which we will find by examining the successive levels of equilibration in the following examples (see Part II).

Let us begin by recalling what we mean by cognitive systems, taking this term in the broadest sense. First, this could mean simple descriptions of observables, *Obs. O* or *S*, conceptualized by the subject on the occasion of an action or of a special event. These systems will also furnish the cognitive instruments used (explicitly or implicitly) by the subject in these conceptualizations—classifications, systems of relations, seriations, numbers, measures, etc.—at every preoperational or operational level. Furthermore, they will provide (this concerns coordinations *Coord. S* and *O*) either the special operational compositions elaborated by the subject on the occasion of the problem posed or his causal explanations. Finally these local compositions, no less than these explanations, will refer to larger structures (groupings, groups, etc.) which constitute the upper level of these various types of systems. This diversity generally allows the boundaries of a cognitive system to remain flexible, regardless of its complexity, except when, in virtue of their specific progressive character, the final operational structures are enclosed within themselves.

2. These principal behaviors should be distinguished according to the relations existing between the modifications and the compensations:

a. When a new fact arises, it can, depending on the situation, produce no modification in the system (for example, an additional object in a classification system prepared to

receive it) or, on the contrary, it can constitute a disturbance (for example, a characteristic which experience reveals and which contradicts a previous description by the
subject, an unexpected object which cannot be placed in a
previously adopted classification system, a perception which
cannot be integrated in a seriation scheme sufficient until
then, etc.). When there are disturbances the reequilibration,
which is produced as a result of the nonbalance, will be
obtained by a behavior known as type a. Consider the following cases.

If there is a small disturbance close to the balancing point,
the compensation will be obtained by a modification introduced by the subject in a direction opposite to the disturbance in question. For example, a young child accustomed
to throwing a ball against another at high speed would be
bothered if we indicated that the impact point had to be
shifted to the side—this for him would constitute a disturbance; if he considered it weak (which is seen from his
behavior), he will compensate it by moving himself so that
he will again face the impact point and continue to throw
the ball at high speed. On the other hand, a second kind of
reaction, of type a, will intervene if the disturbance is
stronger or judged as such by the subject; in this case, he
will cancel the disturbance by neglecting it, or by simply
avoiding it (for example, by displacing the disturbing object in order to place it in a second system). Or if we
experiment with a shock on the side of a ball, we note the
subject will not take this into consideration when throwing
or else he will respect the order and admit that the passive
ball will move in a forward direction as though it were
struck by a moving ball.

When a new characteristic is incompatible with a previous discernment, the subject, though perceiving it, will neglect it or will pretend to consider it, but distort it in order
to adjust it to the scheme retained for the discernment.
(There are innumerable examples: "That moved a bit, nevertheless," the subject will say to explain a mediate transmission, although he will have kept in his hand an immobile

intermediary, etc.). When utilizing classifications, the subject will continue to construct his figurative collection without reworking the previous arrangements.

In situations employing seriation, the child may begin with a pair or a trio (e.g., small, medium, large); then the new elements will be placed in a second trio instead of modifying the first by increasing its extension, etc. It is evident that these type a reactions are only partially compensating, and consequently the resulting equilibriums remain very unstable.

β. Another behavior will consist of integrating into the system the disturbing element arising from without. The compensation then no longer consists in canceling the disturbance or in rejecting the new element, so that it will not intervene within the whole set already organized, but in modifying the system by "equilibrium displacement" so that the unexpected fact is made assimilable. The description will thus be improved; the classification will be recast to coordinate the new category with the others; the seriation will be extended or distributed in two dimensions, etc. Or a causal explanation contradicted by an unexpected fact will be completed or replaced by another explanation which takes the new factor into consideration. In short, what was disturbing became a variation within a reorganized structure, thanks to the new relations which make incorporating the element possible. It is these new characteristics of the structure which ensure the compensation—here again there is definitely a form of compensation.

It is not playing with words to speak here of a compensating mechanism, although now we refer to essentially conceptual compensations which follow the displacement of equilibrium produced by the integration of the disturbance (and which do not yet constitute a compensation as such). The rehandling which is part of the conceptualization modifies, more or less profoundly, the initial system; for example, the subject will substitute for the predicative opposites (such as "small" and "large") reciprocal relations ("more or less large" or "more or less small"), or he will introduce solidarities (such as a perceived unity between the extension and thinning out of a sausage, and inversely between its shortening and the enlargement of its diameter), or in a general way he will reason about the increase or decrease of the values of a function's variables which express any dependency of significance or are inserted in a causal model, etc. In short, by integrating or internalizing the disturbances at play in the cognitive system, these type β behaviors transform them into internal variations which are capable of being compensated, still partially but nevertheless in a manner quite superior to that of type α behaviors.

Let us note, moreover, that these type β compensations extend, in a way, the cancellations of type α (when weak disturbances are involved) by an equal and opposite modification. But here the new modification is not meant to cancel the one which the disturbing object introduces; on the contrary, it alters the assimilation scheme itself to accommodate the object and follows its orientation. In this situation, there is, therefore, equilibrium displacement but with minimization of the cost (as much as possible of the assimilation scheme is conserved and with maximal gain the disturbance is integrated as a new variation in the scheme). In addition, since this integration by scheme accommodation conserves the maximum assimilation compatible with the new variation, the disturbance is eliminated as disturbance.

γ. Superior behavior (which may arise in any logico-mathematical situation and in certain well-elaborated causal explanations) will then consist in anticipating the possible variations which, as foreseeable and deducible, lose their disturbance characteristic and establish themselves in the potential transformations of the system. Thus, for subjects possessing structures for predictions, the projection of a shadow or of a luminous cone, etc., will no longer constitute a disturbance, since it will reenter the transformations capable of being inferred. However, these transformations include a play of compensations but with a fresh significance. Since each transformation can be entirely canceled by its opposite or returned by its reciprocal, in a sense we discover here a situation comparable to that of a disturbing modification and its compensation. The only major difference between these transformations and that of two actions occurring in opposite directions, each tending to cancel the other and reach a compromise (like a balance of two forces), is that, being part of the same system, all the transformations are sufficiently bound together so that the operation T implies the existence of T^{-1} and the product $T \cdot T^{-1} = \iota$. Our understanding of the compensation is consequently that there is a symmetry inherent in the system's organization and no longer an elimination of disturbances.

More precisely, because of the very composition of the structure in play in superior behavior, there is anticipation of all possible transformations. Their symmetry is then due to a complete compensation equal to the "potential work," and the closing of the structure thus eliminates any contradiction emanating from without or from within; however, its intrinsic necessity extends beyond the requirement for mere compensations between opposed but contingent factors.

3. We thus see that there is systematic progress from the first to the second of these behaviors. This is not to say that there are three distinct stages but rather phases which we will discover fairly regularly in the fields studied or in the problems posed at various sensorimotor periods of development—from two through eleven years of age and up to the level required for formal operations. In general these stages enable the equilibration process of cognitive systems to be understood. At every level the systems are based on compensations but their significance is deeply modified and consequently they clearly characterize distinct degrees of equilibrium: the first of these three levels shows unstable equilibrium and a highly restricted field; the second reaction shows equilibrium displacement according to many forms, hence, a great number of possibilities are available for a passage from any level to the following one; and the third type of reaction shows a flexible but stable equilibrium.

In other words, the characteristic of the equilibration of the cognitive systems, as opposed to physical systems, is that they are formed of schemes whose extension and comprehension can be notably enriched by the continuous dual process of assimilation and accommodation which restricts the effects of disturbance and compensating reactions entirely to the levels considered; hence, they become available for possible assimilation: what was a disturbance on the lowest level becomes an internal variation of the system on the highest levels, and what was a compensating reaction which resulted in cancellation finally plays the role of a systematic transforming agent for the variation in play.

The integrations and neutralizations of the initial disturbances consist of retroactive and anticipatory regulations among others, which are the sources of the final reversible operations. Actually, the first of the three kinds of behavior distinguished in section 2 is characterized by the absence of retroactions and anticipations which are necessary to integrate the outside disturbances; hence, we see a series of steps leading closer and closer to integration but simply tending to cancel these disturbances or to displace their effects. With the second type of behavior, the possibility of a retroactive process enables the rehandling or the reorganizations to become more complete so that the point of the neutralization of the disturbances by an integration which incorporates into the system is approached. Any anticipation being a function of previous information, the possibility of anticipation naturally accompanies this step, and new information is furnished by the retroactive "restructurations." Finally the third type of behavior generalizes these anticipations and retroactions in the form of direct and inverse operational compositions. In this case the compensations approached from the preceding level reach a form with complete symmetry and what were initially disturbances are entirely assimilated as internal transformations of the system.

Added to this development of behavior, as illustrated in types a through γ (as shown by the uses of retroactions and anticipations), is the development of differentiations (through gradual accommodation with disturbances) and the internal integration of systems (through assimilation which enriches the cycle which constitutes them). As we have seen in §2 and elsewhere, the relations between the differentiation and the internal integration of the structures constitute a special case of equilibrium which naturally plays an essential role in models of type II in which the increasing number of observables and coordinations pass from state n to $n + 1$, etc., hence, from a to γ, etc.

In his preliminary note on several levels of equilibrium (*Logique et équilibre*, chapter I), Mandelbrot emphasized, among other things, that given linearity of reactions and additivity of minor disturbances, the latter "and the corresponding reactions both form groups of modification of the system, all the elements corresponding one to one: in particular the identities of the two groups are related to one another. This last characteristic will express by definition the reversibility of small disturbances and reactions close to the equilibrium" (page 16). But since Mandelbrot's effort was directed to the finished forms of equilibrium and not to the very process of equilibration, we should remember that for the cognitive systems—and not just any—the modes of compensating reactions differ greatly from one level to the next and above all that the disturbances are conceived by the subject in quite different ways depending on their degree of integration in the system. Here, there is a beginning of reversibility at the outset of elementary regulations, but then only close to the equilibrium point; this reversibility increases with the progress of compensation. Thus it remains legitimate, as we have always emphasized, to consider the reversibility as a result of the equilibration as a complex process which takes in the psychogenetic variations of compensating reactions and modes of comprehension or of disturbance assimilation and not as an independent process called upon to explain the equilibrium.

4. This incorporation of initially disturbing factors— they finally become part of the systems—as well as the in-

ternalization of compensations and their generalization in inverse operations are not solely to be expressed in terms of differentiations and integrations, which are their final effects; their more immediate significance is from their contribution to the fundamental formal process of the equilibration; i.e., the construction of negations in correspondence with affirmations, in other words, the development of reversibility of the operations.

We note that in the reactions of type γ the subject undergoes the rather material external negations (these have not been constructed) formed by the disturbances, and that he replies by negations in action without enrichment of the cognitive system. However, with behaviors of type β the outside disturbance ceases to be entirely negative, since it is incorporated as variation or differences; the construction of partial negations, a new subsystem, or subscheme then corresponds to positive enrichment without the special characteristics of the preceding state but which benefits from participating in its common characteristics. But if this kind of elaboration can begin at the outset of the preoperational levels, their completion naturally implies an adjustment of extensions (quantification of inclusions, etc.) and a "relativization" of predicates which is not achieved at once.

It is with the compensations of type γ that this correspondence of affirmations and negations should finally become systematic; and this should not occur afterward and in more or less extended groping as during β reactions, but according to the virtual compositions included in the operational structures and extended as far as each system operation which has an inverse in one form or other (inversions, reciprocities, or both). Thus the equilibration appears in its first completed forms as compensations between the affirmations and the negations, not only in the relations between the differentiation of parts and the integration into a whole, or in the connections between the subsystems or between the schemes, but also in the elementary relations between the subject and the objects.

§*14/* *Other Possible Formulations of the Equilibration*

We have sought in the preceding text to characterize the relations between the disturbances and the compensating reactions by beginning with a model of virtual modifications in more or less loose analogy with the principle of compensation of potential work used in mechanics. If we wish to turn to other analogies, we can refer to the notions of analytical mechanics in which the equilibrium of a situation is identified by its minimum potential energy,[6] and that of a trajectory by a minimum of action. In terms of cognitive systems—and no longer of physical ones—we could admit that the criterion of "least action" more or less corresponds to that of "least effort," and these are the principles mentioned in the language of metaphysics by Fermat and Maupertuis, who undoubtedly were not unfamiliar with their psychological origin. We can thus consider from such a viewpoint the "economic" or "praxeological" characteristics of compensating reactions by comparing their costs to their gains. In using the term "minimum potential energy," let us be aware of the dangers of any metaphor which refers to energy and limit ourselves to making it correspond in our cognitive systems to the modification power shown by the disturbance factors. Thus, in this new perspective we will no longer question how they are compensated but simply evaluate the extent or importance of the alterations they can create.

1. To continue with this last point, it is clear that it is on the level of type *a* behaviors, defined in § 13, section 2, that the disturbance factors are capable of creating the greatest

---

[6] Let us recall that potential energy should not be confused with the virtual work. A small ball placed on the edge of a table is not in equilibrium because its possible fall corresponds to a positive potential energy and this fall will not be compensated. Once it has fallen into the bottom of a concave container, it will be in equilibrium because its potential energy will be minimum and the virtual work compensates itself.

alterations. As the only forms of equilibrium initially reached concern a very restricted field and remain unstable insofar as their organization continues to be incomplete and neglects a whole set of observables capable of intervening, it is obvious that these observables, precisely to the extent that they are neglected, are the sources of possible great alterations. It is true that compensating reactions exist in these behaviors and function by separating them, but it is not in shifting or distorting them that the subject suppresses their power to cause alterations, and the proof is that they later intervene.

In type β behaviors, the disturbance factors conserve a great modification power as compared to the cognitive system considered but less than in type α, since they are integrated by the compensating reaction and result in changes of equilibrium which retain a part of the initial form and remove from the alterations their disturbance character.

In behaviors of the third type, γ, there are no more disturbing factors, since the system is both flexible and closed, and the outside facts can no longer be sources of contradictions. This is true of the logico-mathematical operational systems and also of causal explanations when they are adequate and when we can make new variations intervene, the possibility of which the explanation virtually admitted.

2. As for the costs and gains characterizing the compensating reactions, or, in other words, the strategies used by the subject to neutralize possible nonbalance, it continues to be very difficult to express them quantitatively in imputation tables characteristic of the theory of play. Nevertheless, we can restrict ourselves to remarks of common meaning and study what clearly seems to be an essential aspect common to the three types of behavior distinguished above and also the notable variations from one type to another.

Behaviors of the first type, α, consist of restricted and weak structures, hence involve little cost, yet allow for no gain from new integrations or compensations. Consequently, during disturbances, the reaction consists only in scattering again what is at once both slightly costly and slightly profitable.

On the other hand, with behaviors of the second type, β, the strategy consists in incorporating the disturbances by a process both retroactive and partially anticipatory, to the extent of making internal variations in the system. In these situations, the cost is a displacement of equilibrium with modifications of the earlier form, but the gain is an extension of the system and, in comprehension, a rehandling of relations with the double benefit of increased coherence and greater safety in handling new disturbances.

With type γ behaviors, the cost is limited to the construction of rules of composition by reflective abstractions, whereas the gain is the whole set of combinations thus rendered possible and protection against any distortion. If we express the combinations in terms of expenses, the strategy will be to minimize the costs—which recalls the "minimum" criterion. In fact, without the system's entire stability, each new composition would give rise to the work of a new adaptation, since the rules of composition would vary. In addition, any communication becomes laborious if instability is not excluded and each partner can use different and unstable processes. Thus it is clear that a stable system of composition reduces to the *maximum* the disturbance risks by using a precorrection procedure whose cost is *minimum*.

3. During a displacement of physical equilibrium with moderation of the disturbance (the Le Châtelier-Braun principle), the partial compensation can include a probable explanation; for example, when a gas is compressed with a piston in a rigid container, there is a great probability of an increase in the molecular movement (heat), hence an increased probability of shocks on the walls (pressure), and finally of piston resistance (moderation of the compression). Likewise, in endocrinology, the equilibration between the incitation leading from the encephalon (brain) to a given gland and the process in the opposite direction can be programmed (the calculation), for an electronic circuit

can be made in terms of well-quantified probabilities. Thus, in considering cognitive systems, it is interesting for us to wonder if the play of successive compensations ensuring the equilibration of hierarchized levels obeys a law of sequential probabilities, as we suggested for our initial 1957 model. But we want to evaluate these possibilities not only as functions of the frequency of encounters (or occurrences) with outside observables or in terms of their power of disturbance, but also as functions of the resistance and flexibility of the particular cognitive system.

The restricted and rigid systems of type a behavior are the ones more likely to be found at the beginning of life because of their limitations. These limitations are due, among other things, to the fact that the multiplicative probability $a \cdot b$ is weaker (if a and b are independent) than those of a or b separately; hence, there is a failure in the relationship between the terms of the covariation and consequently the absence of effective compensations. The probability of a compensation by a simple negation or distortion is, therefore, the strongest at the start of life because of the lack of relational instruments for assimilation and of retroactive or anticipatory mechanisms.

A more interesting problem is created by behaviors of type β. Can we attribute to probability factors the equilibrium displacements when referring to compensation by integration of disturbing elements? A general argument is that the moment a and b are related (and they are the moment b is felt as a disturbance in relation to a, instead of being merely separated), the conditional or multiplicative probability of ab is increased as compared to the state in which they were independent. The regulations at work then render more and more probable the discovery of regular covariations between b and a which sooner or later forces us to differentiate a within the system but as function of b; hence, we have an increasing probability of integration of disturbing variations.

As for the transitions from type β to type γ behaviors, it is evident that insofar as the external disturbances are assimilated in the form of variations within the system, the probability of a complete reversibility ($a.a' = 0$ as compared to $a.a'$ o) increases and the incoherence leads to oscillations (around $a.a' = 0$) which are gradually reduced in their amplitude.

In short, the sequential probabilities and their increase between the α and γ behaviors seem dominated by a double process. On the one hand, by the change of absolute predicates to relations, there is the comprehension of the noncontradiction of qualities or variations which appeared contradictory; hence, the progressive integration of disturbances. On the other hand, there is the elimination of actual contradictions; hence, we see entire reversibility. The first of these processes is then linked to the increasing multiplicative probabilities, whereas the second is linked to the probable reduction of oscillations around the compensation where point $T.T^{-1} = 0$.

II

The Construction
of Structures

Three

A FEW ASPECTS
OF THE DEVELOPMENT
OF SENSORIMOTOR, PERCEPTIVE,
AND SPATIAL STRUCTURES

§*15/* *Constructions, Regulations, and Compensations*

In Bühler's fine posthumous work, published by the Austrian Academy of Science, the great German psychologist explains among other things why the Gestalt theory for him is insufficient to fill the gaps in associationism. The reason, he says, is that it is characteristic of mental life not to reach equilibrium but rather constantly to create relations and instruments of thought. If we conceive of equilibrium in the Gestalt manner as a construct of the constituent factors of a "field," in the physical sense of the term, it is clear that it will be difficult to reconcile such a limited model with the creativity characteristic of the mind's life, since the Gestalt mechanism is assumed to remain the same at every development level. On the other hand, merely to refer to some power of construction would not prove satisfactory unless we furnished the reasons for its productivity. Thus in our work we have consistently turned away from the assumption of predetermined forms of equilibrium to the idea of successive processes of "increasing" equilibration (§6) broken up with nonbalance. Furthermore, we have predicated that the passage of the nonbalance, or of imperfect froms of equilibrium to "better" forms, implies at each stage the intervention of new constructions, themselves determined by the requirements of compensations and reequilibrations. In such a model the equilibrium and the creativity are thus more antagonistic but closely interdependent.

In the following pages, the construction is expressed as a function of interactions of type I and II (§9 to §12), whereas the various form of equilibrium correspond to the a, β, or γ type behaviors (§13) which by their compensating reactions in turn correspond to the disturbances (or nonbalances) opposing these constructions. But if this conciliation is to be substantiated, we must prove with the facts that level by level the progressive relations between the observables and the resultant coordinations require multiple but gradual compensations. In other words, now we must establish the necessary correspondence between the various relations involving observables, or the various varieties of constructive coordinations (as inferences) and the multiple forms of compensations.

The interpretation which we are going to develop by extending the propositions of Chapter One thus means admitting that if any construction, at any level, tends to reach a form of equilibrium that we can consider internal as compared to the system, the reason is that, at the outset, this construction plays a compensation role for certain disturbances. Such a role can be verified by analysis of the regulations intervening during the construction. In other words, we will rediscover the general process which in each situation—with certain exceptions—will begin with the exercise of a scheme of assimilation whose activation will sooner or later be hindered by disturbances. The resulting compensations will then be expressed by a new construction whose regulations—those characterizing these phases—will thus be both compensating in respect to the disturbances (by thus implying at least the potential formation of negations) and formative as compared to the construction. This process will continue until a new balanced structure is attained, and the development of similar processes has begun. As for the initial scheme, either it must be acquired and thus stem from a similar but previous development, or it must be innate and therefore be a product of regulations or compensations of organic origin.

Before seeking to justify this conception, let us again note that it represents a possible synthesis of genetic structuralism, all our previous work, and the functionalism evident in the work of Dewey, Claparède, and in many aspects of Freudian psychoanalysis. According to the functionalist perspective, any mental activity, especially cognitive, proceeds from a tendency to satisfy a need resulting from a momentary nonbalance by establishing a reequilibration. The need is expressed in the form of "interests," and these show two inseparable aspects. On the one hand, the interest indicates a relation between the subject's needs and the object's characteristics—the latter is "interesting" insofar as it meets the needs (compensation). On the other hand, according to Claparède, interest is a dynamic generator which liberates the subject's energy and animates action in the object's direction, thereby regulating positive feedback. This is reminiscent of the notions of energy as "cathexis" and "loads" suggested by Freud.

In our interpretation of the connections between any cognitive construction and outside disturbances with their resultant compensating reactions (the role of construction is to produce them), it goes without saying that an essential place should be reserved for need and consequently for interests. On the one hand, interest is the motivating force or value in any assimilation scheme, an object being of interest for this scheme insofar as it can feed the interest. (D. Rapaport, the best theoretician of psychoanalysis, in his studies on *attention-cathexis*, stressed the relationship—which appeared clear to him—between the cathexis and our notion of a feeding of assimilation schemes.) On the other hand, need is the expression of a scheme's momentary non-functioning, and, from the cognitive viewpoint, it thus corresponds to a gap or a deficit, that is, to a negative aspect of the disturbances. In short, as we have suggested in §5, the concepts of nonbalance and reequilibration permit the possibility of a connection between the functionalist viewpoint and that which is characteristic of our genetic structuralism.

§16/   *The Sensorimotor Regulations*

To analyze the regulations intervening in the recording of observables and their relations (see the *Obs. S* and *Obs. O* interactions of type II, §10–12) and to verify that they orient the constructions submitted to them toward compensations, we must return to the sensorimotor levels. Indeed, in a great number of cases observed in detail, we have found that the subject succeeds in constructing certain relations and in obtaining certain results or performances by carrying out simply practical sensorimotor actions without being conscious of the means employed. Let us recall that consciousness is not at all limited to being aware of the action's mechanisms, so that no other insights are added; on the contrary, consciousness consists in internalizing the actions in the form of representations, that is, interpreting them by means of conceptualizations which can be more or less adequate. Since what we called "observables" in the interactions of type II) are related to this conceptualization, we are again presented with the problem of how to identify the actual sensorimotor regulations. We must determine whether their methods are analogous, but less developed because of their elementary character, to those of higher levels or whether they constitute processes oriented in a different manner.

1. First of all, let us note that the initial assimilation schemes are innate, few in number, and very generous in their coverage of assimilable fields. They include sucking (a scheme which rapidly effects more than the limited feeding periods), looking, listening, and touching (with the palmar reflex and later an increasingly extended activation leading to intentional prehension). The disturbances, which could hinder the exercise of these schemes, will first consist of simple gaps (unsatisfied momentary needs, lack of real sucking, etc.[1]). In a second phase—the transition between the preceding and the third—the disturbance is linked to what we could call the space-time distances between the assimilable object and the subject; for example, the object studied emerges from a visual field, or a modification of the entire perceptual field replaces the overall picture in which the assimilation took place. Finally, in a third phase only and rather late (toward stage IV of our six sensorimotor stages[2]), the disturbance is due to a well-delimited and manipulated object or event. Since it is only in the third phase that we again find situations comparable, from the viewpoint of the significance of disturbances and compensations, to those analyzed in Part I of this work, it is essential to keep in mind this evolution of disturbances in order to judge the nature of the compensating regulations.

A second fundamental fact dominates the entire development of sensorimotor behaviors. If we use our understanding of interactions of types IIA through C (§10 through 12), we note that during the first stages (and precisely at those levels where the disturbances are of a primi-

---

[1] But on this level from the outset we observe compensations; for example, the vacuum sucking which recalls the *Leerlauf* which K. Lorenz has pointed out as being an instinct among animals.

[2] See *La naissance de l'intelligence chez l'enfant*, and *La construction du réel chez l'enfant*. Stage I is that of reflexes and spontaneous movements, stage II that of first habits, stage III that of secondary circular reactions, stage IV that of the coordination of means and ends, stage V that of the discovery of means, and stage VI that of inventions by sudden comprehension.

tive type) the observations made on the objects (*Obs. O*) and on the action itself (*Obs. S*) remain essentially un- differentiated. For example, the infant, before considering his hands as organs dependent on him or on his intentions and as parts of his body, a well-delimited system itself, looks at them as though they were foreign entities crossing his visual field and can even become frightened when these undirected objects happen to touch his face. Or when he takes a solid object to his mouth to suck it, he has no knowl- edge of this mouth or head, except through tactile-kines- thetic or gustative channels, and by no means does he pic- ture to himself the space-time path according to which the object approaches his mouth. Thus at the initial level of the sensorimotor development, only overall observables exist, which we can call *Obs. OS*. There are no observables re- lated to the objects insofar as the objects are inseparable from the characteristics which link them to the body itself (for example, an object to suck, etc.), or related to the subject's actions, since he does not know his actions as such, does not perceive the details, and ignores everything about himself as well as his body. Actually he does not yet form a subject, any more than he conceives objects as permanent, localizable, etc.[3]

It goes without saying that at the start no differentiations could exist which would make it possible to distinguish the coordinations between actions (*Coord. S*), and between ob- jects (*Coord. O*). The first reason is that the causal coordi- nations between objects clearly appear much later than

---

[3] It should be noted that we classify the schemes for the "ob- servables" in the sense of §8 and not for the coordinations, since the latter are based on inferences considered necessary. A special scheme, although not being perceived as a scheme, is shown by analogies when the child assimilates an object to himself. As for what we eventually call coordinations between schemes, they constitute the elementary form of coordinations, for while merely beginning from inductive inferences (for example, a sonorous observable making it possible to anticipate the presence of a visual observable), they produce a causal link which intervenes the moment the prehension occurs.

between the subject's actions and the objects; this is one of the decisive lessons to be learned about the sensorimotor period—Michotte's studies of visual causality changes nothing, for it is based on the tactile-kinesthetic causality tied to the subject's actions. Second, if the coordinations linking the subject's actions and objects thus appear prior to these *Coord. O* proper, at first, before the subject succeeds in regulating in detail his own actions, they use only *Obs. OS.* (Eventually they permit the beginning of awareness insofar as this adjustment implies choices or a certain "vigilance.") Third, these early coordinations based on *Obs. OS* (which at first merely consist of reciprocal assimilations between schemes) are not themselves immediate and only begin at stage II during which the first habits are acquired; at stage I no coordination is observed between schemes or actions.

2. In other words, before we can present the processes in conformity with the general model IIA of §10, section 6, the beginning of this equilibration may be represented by the following form:

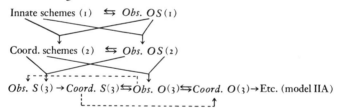

The passage from these initial reactions to type IIA interactions (through every intermediary that we can distinguish in detail) corresponds to a rather radical transformation which we have often commented upon and which we have compared to a kind of Copernican revolution; during the first months of existence, the infant's universe consists of changing scenes with no permanent objects or causality between objects, and without the subject being aware of it, he is entirely centered on his body and its action. This is obvious, as before the coordinations, *Coord. S₃*, there is not even a differentiated subject. During the second year, however, body and action are situated in the time-space of a coherent universe and, among other perceptions, his body is recognized as a permanent object and center of causality. Now, this total reversal of perspectives, leading to such a radical egocentrism that a decentered system of interdependent and intelligible transformations is completely ignored, is due first of all to the differentiation of observables OS in observables of the action itself ($Obs.\ S$), and of the objects ($Obs.\ O$), and consequently to the differentiated coordinations ($Coord.\ S$ and $Coord.\ O$) which are made possible by this differentiation. The problem then—and we will see that it was with us from the beginning—is to determine if this vast construction, whose contribution to the eventual development of cognitive functions in their entirety is considerable, is due to equilibration by compensations and if the regulations at work here are significant. This is the first and a highly significant example of general equilibrium between the differentiation of subsystems of schemes or of separate parts and the integration of the whole which compensates it and leads to the decentralization just recalled. We must now consider the details of the regulations, at first as independent functions, then within the overall integration.

3. With the very establishment of innate schemes we see the forming of certain regulations. If we consider sucking, for example, we can state that it is steadier after a few days than at the beginning and that, most obviously, the infant finds the nipple more easily if by chance he lets go of it. In this predicament, the infant tends to rediscover the nipple by turning in a direction opposite from that in which it was withdrawn from the child's mouth or makes movements back and forth of decreasing width. Thus here we see a driving regulation ensuring a compensation of type a (for weak disturbances see §13, section 2). A similar pattern expresses the activity of looking; if an object sighted by the subject is moved out of the visual field, a slight movement of the head or eyes displaces this field until the object is again found in its center (again we have a compensation of type a).

As for the earliest habits (acquired by primary circular

reactions) which actually constitute the elementary constructions, these consist of novel actions which are integrated into innate schemes as they continue to be performed: thumb sucking by systematic adduction and no
longer by chance, rediscovering with a glance an object that
has left the visual field (by extension of the ocular-cephalic
reflex), etc. We must not merely consider the completed
and consolidated states, but study the regulations which
preside at the formation of such habits, and understand that
the compensations do more than satisfy momentary needs.
We note that at the beginning the reactions consist in put-
ting the thumb back in the mouth when it has just opened
after a fortuitous encounter, in continuing reflex movement
when an object followed by the eyes has just disappeared,
etc. Here again are compensations of type a, but these are
extended fully by the progressive regulations.

We now turn to acquisitions by conditioning. We know
that they raise the pretty problem of equilibrium, since a
conditioned behavior is stable only when "confirmed" peri-
odically by presentation of the absolute stimulation after
the reception of the conditional stimulus. Thus it is clear
that so-called "association" is actually an assimilation which
confers a significance to a signal by incorporating it in a
scheme on which need and satisfaction depend, and that the
characteristic of the regulation imposed during the course
of training is the division of this satisfaction (hence, the
feeding of the scheme) into two stages due to a temporary
replacement of the food with its announcement and expec-
tation. In this case, the disturbance by gap or modification
of the time-space distance (see section 1) is compensated by
a replacement or a modification in the opposite direction
(substitution). Using our interpretations, the signal itself
would do more than indicate a feeding; it would be directly
assimilated as an aspect or part of the entire initial "food +
signal" configuration through a kind of pure and simple
replacement of the absolute stimulus by the conditioned
response.

4. The chief problem at the next level concerns the co-

ordination between schemes. The most precocious forms are those which link vision and hearing (i.e., looking in the direction of a sound to find the corresponding visual image), then sucking and prehension (i.e., bringing to the mouth what is clutched and not part of the visual field). Most importantly (at four or five months) there is coordination of vision and prehension (i.e., grasping what is seen, taking what is reached before the eyes without the help of vision, and looking in the direction of a hand holding it). Here is a reciprocal assimilation of different schemes, and the explanation is simple. Since there are frequent situations where one object can be both seen and heard, sucked or touched and seen close by, then held in the hand which brushed it, these intersections of schemes produce or leave a gap when one of them is activated without the other; that is, an object heard *without* being seen requires being seen, etc. (and later an object seen and grasped will be shaken to discover if it produces a sound). From our observation of the development of regulations through groping during the acquisition of these coordinations (which probably intervene at the outset of the maturation of the neural connections making the reciprocal assimilations possible), the process appears as follows: starting from a situation with an intersection in which the objects considered present both x and y characteristics, a contrary situation may arise where the objects are perceived as x without y or y without x and which is characterized by a time-space distance between x and y (i.e., an object may emerge in the visual field yet not be heard, felt by the hands, seen, etc.); then the disturbance created by this distance is compensated by a movement in the opposite direction which links x and y. (These compensations are again of type a; see §13, section 2.)

Thus these coordinations constitute the source of new schemes, xy, which are available in addition to schemes of characteristics x or y. This results in the possibility of secondary circular reactions which will produce many others by differentiation from the multiplicative schemes xy. For example, a subject attempting to grasp a suspended object will strike it and fail to surround it with his hand and, now interested in an unusual sight, created by chance, will attempt to find it again by a reciprocal assimilation actually consisting of a series of regulations or corrections carried on until stabilization of success is secured. From the viewpoint of equilibrium and relations between disturbances and compensations, a paradox becomes evident. The new event, which is the striking of the object, doubtless represents, during at least a short period, a disturbance in relation to the subject's intention, which was merely to grasp the object. Nevertheless there is an immediate transfer of interest by substitution, and the supposed disturbance immediately seems integrated by a behavior announcing a type β interaction (§13) into the general scheme; the action consists of displacing the object by means of the hands and becomes constitutive of a differentiated subscheme. Here therefore is the question: How is the immediate interest in the disturbing event formed and then transferred into a strongly desired goal? (We recall Preyer's son raising a box cover 119 times, then letting it fall; this also resulted from an initial disturbance.)

The solution to this question—and this applies again at the most evolved stages—is apparent when we remember the relative characteristic of the notion of disturbance; e.g., for a scientist who holds to a theory an unexpected fact is a disturbance, whereas for another, whose aim is to revise it, the same fact is at once assimilable. Let us recall two fundamental aspects of the beginnings of sensorimotor activity. The first is the very general nature of the schemes used; during coordination of vision and prehension, the essential goal is not so much to grasp the object as to exercise on it the powers of the hand, such as displacing, making contact, etc., and if the hand balances it, this power extension is not a disturbance but an unexpected specification. Second, at these elementary levels, there is as yet no differentiation or boundaries between the world of objects (there is a lack of substantial permanency) and that of actions or of powers of the self (there is precisely a lack of a "self"). The balancing of the suspended object is thus merely an *Obs. SO*, that is, an undifferentiated power which belongs both to the object and to the subject. It is to be expected, therefore, that the regulation released by this event tends to reproduce it and conserve it (positive feedback) and not to cancel it as it would a disturbance. Let us not hasten, then, to draw conclusions during the early appearance of a compensation by integration (type β behavior, see §13), since in the present example there was no previous cancellation behavior to be followed by integration, and let us limit ourselves to seeing here a transition behavior resulting from scheme coordinations and announcing the tertiary circular reactions which are of type β.

5. We must now recall the first examples observed in our earlier studies regarding the level of differentiations and coordinations between means and goals (stage IV): removing a cushion which hinders the hand's movements from reaching an object or placing an adult's hand in the direction of the object which is too far away for the child. It is clear that the first of these behaviors consists in compensating a disturbance by shoving aside a disturbing object; in the second, the subject uses the adult's hand to compensate by its movement a space-time distance disturbing direct prehension. It should be noted that in the first of these cases, we observe a beginning of negations constructed by the subject, whereas in the second the negations are imposed by the object.

As for the object's permanency which is established shortly afterward, it develops as a function of these same two methods. At the preceding levels, when, at the moment it is going to be grasped, the desired object is hidden by a screen, there is of course disturbance yet without compensation because the universe is still perceived as a series of overall pictures and an object belonging to one picture may be merely reabsorbed and not return in the following picture. When, on the contrary, the very widespread compensations of the first levels are replaced by coordinations and multiplications of schemes (see section 4) and intelligent behaviors coordinating means and goals, the compensating regulations which differentiate then consist in compensating the disturbing space-time distances by actions in the opposite direction and in displacing an obstacle in order to cancel its intervention. In our example, the screen which hides the desired object is no longer bound up with an entirely new, overall picture but is conceived as a moving object whose arrival can be corrected by being shoved aside. Likewise, the object's successive positions during its disappearances are gradually included as compensable space-time distances. After being neglected the object attains a greater importance because the action of finding it again has succeeded for the first time. In short, perceiving the possibility of rejoining the object by displacing the screen, and the increasing comprehension of the reversibility of displacements, are merely manifestations of a generalization of compensating regulations which will greatly modify behaviors during stages V and VI.

But what is the driving force of this generalization? First, let us recall that the compensations by cancellation (see type a behaviors in §13) can acquire two distinct forms, depending on whether they are the results of minor or major disturbances; with the first, the disturbing displacement is corrected by a displacement in the opposite direction, whereas if the disturbance is important it is merely avoided or neglected. When objects disappear behind a screen, the disturbance is conceived as important or widespread because the subject has few schemes and the desired sensitive modification of effects appears bound up with a complete change of the entire picture; in this situation, the subject does not know what to compensate and gives up. As the schemes increase and allow for connections from means to goals, this change of scale for items dealt with refines the regulations, and what appeared as an important disturbance becomes related to the modifications of details or places which the more numerous schemes make it possible to achieve. It is then that the intervention of a screen is considered a weak disturbance because it is partial and is compensable by the reverse modification. From the viewpoint of negations, this change of perspective is important; whereas the simple picture change merely involves differences, removing the screen, conceived of as an obstacle, again involves a negation (although entirely practical) constructed by the subject.

6. Level IV shows the coordination of means and goals which marks the beginning of intelligent acts proper, and the first forms of the perception of object permanency; in addition, it inaugurates the second period of sensorimotor development during which we witness—and shall see more and more on levels V and VI—the progressive equilibration of differentiations and integrations which finally takes into account the complete reversal of perspectives just mentioned. We must now study the details starting with compensating regulations. In principle this equilibration merely constitutes a vast extension of the equilibrated relations between the accommodation (the source of differentiations) and the reciprocal assimilation between the subsystems (the source of complete integration), but both are achieved by means of many partial regulations.

First, it goes without saying that with polarity between the subject and the objects, introduced when substantial permanency is attributed to the objects, the accommodations will become more precise; that is, they will accompany more advanced compensating regulations, since now reactions are differentiated from individual objects existing as such in a stable manner and no longer from the overall and changing pictures. Hence, we have more differentiated accommodations from the relations between means and goals. But object permanency goes hand in hand with that of persons. Persons even constitute the first permanent objects and give rise from the affective viewpoint to these "object relations" whose link with this permanency we have shown. As J. M. Baldwin has correctly seen, the formation of the self is linked to these interpersonal relations, notably to imitation, which, as we have suggested, constitutes an extension of accommodations (with all the detailed regulations present at its acquisition). Not only at the subject's pole but at the object's; therefore, one finds the first substantial set of differentiations bound up with accommodations, with all the compensations they include, and with the negations they imply.

Second, we witness at stage V new behaviors also stemming from accommodations to the object and constituting a second important differentiation factor; these are the tertiary circular, or "to see experience," reactions with factor variations. They produce modifications which, until this level, would have been regarded as disturbing. Thus, at the beginning of the sensorimotor period, but at the level involving only physical action without conceptual representation, we witness behaviors of type a change into type β reactions (§13) by the integration of disturbances into the appropriate cognitive system, and even by the intentional variation of factors which thus cease to be disturbing through the use of compensating accommodations. Here it should be noted that the production of more or less systematic variations (for example, dropping or throwing a ball higher or less high, with more or less strength, to the left or to the right, etc.), are evident as positive or negative physical differences in the parameters of the action.

Next we consider a third important set of differentiations which extend the preceding and play an important role in the conquest of the world of objects. This is the discovery of means; for example, using an intermediary object such as a carpet, a string, or an instrument proper, such as a stick, to bring a distant object to oneself. In studying compensating regulations, nothing is more instructive than following the beginnings of such behaviors: for example, one can watch the kind of substitution which at the outset leads to concerning oneself with a tool in place of the goal which is at too great a distance, then see the corrections in movement made to achieve the goal, etc.

A whole set of assimilating coordinations gradually develops to correspond to these sets of differentiations, leads to integrations, and prevents this multiplicity of differentiated behavior from resulting in disorder or in the simple juxtaposition of reactions without connections. Once objects have become permanent, we first see the coordination of positions and displacements occurring during the course of stages V and VI in the great space-time system of physical displacements; without representing the whole, although getting closer and closer, this system confers on the sensorimotor universe a remarkable unity of decentered structures. Next we note the casuality which, magical and phenomenological at its beginnings (since it is linked solely to the special actions of a subject who knows nothing of it), occurs in space and objectifies itself by becoming the interaction system between the objects themselves. Finally it is the whole set of reciprocal assimilations between the schemes or between the subsystems related to the subject himself which makes coordination between objects possible.

It is evident that each of these integrations reveals two kinds of increasing equilibrations. On the one hand, in any particular situation a whole set of regulations is necessary to establish these coordinations, and for a group of displacements they are especially clear during groping which leads to the acquisition of return behaviors (group reversibility) and of detours (group associativity). On the other hand, a more general process of equilibration intervenes between the differentiations and the integrations in the sense that each accommodation, the source of differentiated novelties, corresponds to an assimilation which links it to more or less general coordinations; without these links the differentiations would be both chaotic and without durable effect.

This reexamination of sensorimotor regulations seems to furnish the first justification of our general proposition: that the genesis of constructions superposing themselves level by level is not foreign to the compensating mechanisms, since the elaboration of each of these structures begins with a phase of regulations which are at the same time compensating and formative. We can even claim that the novelty of a behavior (and when one sees the number of conquests obtained in eighteen months it seems likely that during the sensorimotor period these innovations succeed one another most rapidly) is proportional to the importance of the disturbances that are necessary for compensation. The use of the stick, for example, which constitutes the first of these behaviors so essential in the development of practical intelligence and causality, begins with a complex set of compensations. To replace the objective distance with an extension of the arm, to correct the disorderly displacements during the first contact of the stick with the object, to rectify the undesirable motions with thrusts in the opposite direction, and finally to reduce the distance by a sufficiently adjusted adduction, are a series of compensating regulations whose entire richness could only be shown by a slow motion film.[4]

It is clear that the formal aspect of these regulations is expressed, among other things, by the formation of multiple negations which, although remaining at the action level, will constitute the source of abstractions destined later to play their role in the laborious construction of conceptualized negations.

§17/ *The Perceptive Regulations*

The observables *Obs. S*, which we dealt with in the first part of this work (type II interactions), all imply a previous action on the part of the subject whose basic methods are of a sensorimotor type. Thus it is worthwhile verifying that at the outset of the development of sensorimotor levels the structural constructions proceed by increasingly finer compensations. The gaps ordinarily noticed in the elementary forms of these observables (see Chapter Two) are instructive, since they are situated at the level of the conceptualization proper and not of its sensorimotor regulation. Consequently, the gradual equilibration of these *Obs. S* (with the

---

[4] See the work by P. Mounoud, *Structuration de l'instrument chez l'enfant*, Delachaux, 1970.

attendant *Obs. O* and the *Coord. S* and *O*) includes new
processes and a whole reconstruction on the superior level,
which is that of awareness or conceptualization. But these
observables related to the subject's activities and a fortiori
those related to the objects (*the Obs. O*) imply in addition
an adequate perception. The problem posed is to establish if
they are well perceived or if not why they fail to find a
remedy in the perceptive mechanisms if the insufficiencies
can show up at the beginning. It is equally necessary, in
order to reach a valid interpretation of regulation dealing
with these conceptualized observables, to reexamine the
question of perceptive regulations and to discover whether
they suffice or are unable to deal with these observables
adequately.

The fact that an equilibration of perception exists, and
consequently a play of regulations characteristic of this
field, is shown by the existence of certain perceptions useful
for learning or improvement which involve no recourse
whatever to external reinforcements. We must begin with
such facts and not with the notion of equilibrium characteristic of Gestalt theory in which analysis is not psychogenetic and in which explanation refers too rapidly to physical
field models without construction of temporary intermediary stages (as would be suggested by thermodynamic
analogies), or active regulations (since on a "field" there is
no subject, and regulation is both automatic and instantane-
ous).

When we present subjects of different ages with the same
configuration source of systematic illusion, often in immediate succession (as in the experiments done at our request by Noelting using the Müller-Lyer figure, and as also
found in the work of Ghoneim showing the underestimation of the diagonal of a diamond-shaped object), we observe rather different reactions according to the development level. Until about the age of seven the illusion,
measured during each successive presentation (by an adjustment method, scarcely strict but rapid), does not
change quantitatively but simply oscillates around an aver-

age constant for each subject. From the ages of seven to twelve, we witness a gradual and rather significant improvement for almost every subject, and for the population as a whole an even greater improvement which increases rather rapidly each year—weak at seven, it gradually approaches adult reaction. In general with adults the improvement is strong, and certain subjects achieve a complete cancellation of the illusion, although naturally not one of them (at any age) is informed of his performances, measure by measure. Let us note, in addition, that the illusion itself, regardless of repetitions, weakens with age, which is doubtless due to the effects of learning; if this were not true the improvement with repetition of the exercise should be greater with young subjects, since they begin with a stronger illusion.

These results are instructive from at least two viewpoints. First, they show that beginning at a certain level (seven years) the sustained exploration of a perceived configuration diminishes the distortions by a variety of spontaneous compensations (since there is no external reinforcement from information on the results obtained). If these distortions are due to the effects of attention centration, as we have attempted to show (according to the probability of "encounters" between vision and the perceived elements of the object and of "pairings" between these encounters), this would mean that in multiplying the centration points, the perceptual exploration would lead to a compensation of the actions (by making the "pairings" complete). In other words, the reduction of distortions inherent in the immediate interaction of elements in each field of centration (i.e., the whole set of relations perceived simultaneously) would be due to the activities proper (here the exploration), and include a regulating mechanism.

Second, these regulations develop with age. When studying the movements and centrations of looking at a figure, as we have done with Ving Bang, we note that young subjects choose their points of fixation poorly and thus know relatively little of how to explore a configuration systematically.

Thus the exploring activity improves with age, and if we look for the reasons, it is difficult to escape the proposition according to which, in addition to the visual perception which more or less adequately records what is seen, there is a superior urge which decides what should be centered so that the eyes take in the greatest amount of information. In other words, it is not enough to "see" in the sense of visually perceiving; one needs "to know how to see" in the sense of choosing properly what should be seen. Since progress in the exercises of learning described above is significant only beginning at the age of seven and regularly increases with the cognitive development, we are forced to admit that this urge or guidance depends on whole structures constructed during this evolution, which in the large sense means intelligence. It is important to note that this guiding of exploratory activities by intelligence also presents compensations which simply reinforce those of the lower levels. On the centration level each perception is distorted, but two distinct and successive centrations partly compensate each other. On the middle level, the perceptual exploration tends to cover the principal parts of the figure in order gradually to reduce the distortions. On the third level, the intervention of intelligence consists simply in choosing the points of maximum compensation, which furnish the most information with the least possible loss.

2. Along with perceptual activities, whose success is relatively late, there are others which also evolve with age (and thus do not contradict what precedes) but are formed much earlier, and from the outset present certain compensating methods. Such are the perceived constancies of size and form, etc., each of which shows a remarkable play of compensations. Thus the size of a receding object is perceived according to actual dimensions despite the diminishing of the retinal image, and hence of the apparent or projected size. This decrease is compensated by the increase in the distance to the object, as though perception corrected the apparent size as a function of this distance. The proof of this is that we find in certain experimental situations that if

young subjects (and again up to the age of seven) some-what underestimate sizes at a distance, they then overesti-mate sizes at a distance.[5] With certain adults the over-estimation can be considerable, as though their compensat-ing method was reinforced by a precaution, by a strategy against error. To achieve constancy of forms, the per-ceptual distortion which appears when we modify an ob-ject's position is compensated by a correction directed by the "normal" or originally seen position (facing, etc.).

These constancies, with the compensating regulations they include, are built up at the start of the sensorimotor period, and present work seems to show them even more advanced than we had thought. This leaves open the pos-sibility of an innate point of departure. But, even if such an innate origin existed, this initial method would not suffice for all constancies (for there always exists a necessary solidarity between maturation and training), and two facts cannot be questioned. The first is that (despite the Gestalt theorists) there is an improvement in constancies with the development of cognitive functions, and sometimes this continues even up to the superconstancies or supercompen-sations that are found. The second fact is that, beginning at the sensorimotor level, interactions exist between these perceptual constancies and intelligence, for example, be-tween the constancy of form and permanency of an ob-ject.[6]

[5] For example, a vertical rod measuring 8–9 cm at a distance of 4 m would be perceived as though it measured 10 cm.

[6] And there is more. An innate device can give rise either to an unvarying reply to a stimulus, like sucking movements of the mouth in contact with the breast, or to graduated replies which then con-tinue in acquired regulations, for example, the ocular-cephalic reflex which responds to a more or less rapidly moving object. Here the hereditary reaction is already compensating at various degrees. The precocious constancies of perception of size observed by Bower cause the intervention of the parallax of the head's movements, whereas neither the binocular parallax nor perspective or recovering, etc., as yet seem to play a role. What appears to furnish the innate method would therefore already be a functioning of possible regulations

It is clear that we must admit a certain convergence between the compensating methods at work in the formation of perceptual constancies and those we pointed out (§19) in the development of operational conservations (which includes the increasing correspondence of variations in quantity, direction, intensity, etc.). This homology is valuable in understanding the generality of the processes of equilibration characteristic of the cognitive functions. But it is equally evident that conservations are not derived from constancies, since seven years separate these two constructions. The conservations are inherent in the transformations of the object itself, whereas the constancies merely deal with the results of the modifications of position or distance between the subject and the object. The perceptual regulation is capable of making the compensating corrections, but would not suffice to compensate a real modification of objects. Even in achieving constancy of colors when objects seem modified by lighting, the play of compensations deals merely with the relations between the perception of the lighted object's reflective power (albedo) and that of the light intensity.

3. Our problem is to establish whether the regulations dealing with the observables in play in interactions of types I and II (§9 to 12) are reducible to regulations of percep-

---

although they are very incomplete. It goes without saying that the assumption of innateness scarcely modifies the terms of the problem. Although the ocular-cephalic reflex does not explain the search for the object which is outside the visual field (either immediately or after a long time), nor the permanency of objects, it does constitute the point of departure of a series of increasingly complex acquisitions. In like manner, hereditary constancies, if they exist, merely furnish an initial stage for subsequent constructions. The question posed, since the constancies would already be regulating (including the physiological homeostasis), is whether the compensations intervening in their functioning are regulated step by step by heredity or whether at the outset of this stage general laws of equilibration intervene. We know in fact that these laws are found at every biological level and even apply, at the general level, to a previous condition and are not a result of the biogenetic transmission.

tion, while remembering that, despite the remarkable generality and the analogies of the forms of compensating methods between the two levels of perception and intelligence, sooner or later perception must be summoned to complete intelligence. The subject needs to constantly know what to look at (listen to, or touch, etc.) in order to achieve a certain objectivity and to reduce the perceptual distortions—an unguided perception being insufficient to entirely fulfill its recording function.

It may perhaps be useful to give three examples in which inference made at superior levels guides perception. In these special examples, the inferences furnish the perceptual activities with exploratory mechanisms which they would not have found alone, whereas in the preceding examples, the guidance of intelligence limits itself to completing the compensating processes already at work in the perceptual mechanisms.

The first of these examples refers to the possibility of perception of the "horizontality" or the "verticality" of a straight line. We know that these notions, insofar as they are conceptual and operational, are only developed at about nine or ten years of age, although perception of these directions, with fair success, is attained by referring to the particular line and the position of the body. However, in situations which present conflicts, we note the existence of more complex reactions. For example, we may present a triangle whose base is sloped and within which we have drawn a straight line. The subject is called upon to perceive if the line is horizontal or not. The youngest children give relatively good replies, neglecting the triangle itself (compensation by cancellation!). Children aged five to eight or nine are progressively disturbed by the triangle and errors increase because of lack of compensations. At about the age of nine or ten, however, they begin to seek references beyond the triangle, or between figures, and look at the edges of the sheet which is equipped with a large and visible frame. Why at this age? The examination of the same subjects by means of the usual operational proof (prevision of the horizontality of a water level in a jar, after stating that we are going to slope it) shows a close correlation but with a slight advance in intelligence. In other words, guidance by intelligence was required in order for perception to be turned to clues outside the triangle which compensate the distorting effects of the triangle.

A second example concerns the relations between the operational transitivity and the perceptual transposition. We present two vertical rods, each 10 cm in length; rod C is placed at a distance and rod A is placed close by. Then we measure the error in depth perception (size constancy) which in general indicates underestimation by subjects up to the ages of seven or eight and an overestimation beyond. We next place a rod B (also 10 cm) near A and then near C, and with B in the latter position we take a new measure of C and compare it to A. Finally we question the subject on the transitivity $A = C$, if $A = B$ and $B = C$. The subjects under seven years of age who lack this operational transitivity make errors during the second experiment equal to those made in the first. Subjects aged nine and older make no further errors after the intervention of B. Subjects aged seven to nine who already have the transitivity still show a perceptual but weak error; "I know that $A = C$," one says, "but I see it a bit smaller." Thus in this experiment we note an advance and the guiding action of intelligence on the regulation of perception. This is apparent even in an area as precociously regulated as size constancy.

A third example comes from the perception of serial configurations. We present a subject with about thirty parallel vertical lines arranged according to length—with equal increments between their lengths (simple seriation) or with decreasing differences (parabola). We ask the subject to compare the differences between two neighboring elements toward the beginning of the series (between the second and third line), toward the end (between the twenty-fifth and twenty-sixth line), or between other pairs. Young subjects limit themselves to direct compositions and commit various errors, whereas older subjects cross the virtual line of the summits and thus correct their estimates.

We note to what degree the regulations and perceptual conpensations, although analogous in their forms to those of the preoperational levels and often even operational levels (constancies and conservations) of intelligence, remain insufficient to achieve a complete recording of observables. In fact, the conceptualization of the observables naturally could not be taken solely from perception, and—this is less evident—in many cases it is this conceptualization itself that orientates the perceptual activities and leads the subject to perceiving what he would not have seen otherwise as well as compensating for the distortions inherent in the unguided perception.

§ *18/ The Spatial Regulations*

Before turning to the study of regulations dealing with the observables and the coordinations of general characteristics which intervene in our models of type I and II interactions (§9–12), it is useful to complete the preceding introductory discussion by reviewing briefly the questions of space construction, but now we must give more attention to the compensating regulations which earlier we had partly neglected.

1. When the sensorimotor space, mentioned in §16, and the perceptual space begin to be completed on a new level by the representative space, we note with some surprise that the sensorimotor coordinations which intervene in behavior involving the use of instruments (supports, stick, etc.), and physical displacements, the proper forms and perceptual constancies which already include, on this elementary level, an entire Euclidian and projective geometry, nothing similar corresponds in the first spatial representations. Hence, there is no correspondence on the level of verbal or even graphic conceptualization. All that is retained are the

topological characteristics of enclosure, continuity, closeness, and separation, i.e., boundaries (with closing and opening, or internalization and externalization) and beginnings of order.

We will not review an experiment discussed in much detail elsewhere,[7] but recall that the initial primacy of this representative topology has been contested because the distinction of the linear or curvilinear lines is always precocious and seems to be Euclidian in nature. In a fine study of the qualitative and statistical control of our results, M. Laurendeau and A. Pinard[8] verified the topological primacy and showed that the apparently Euclidian distinction which had remained in question could itself be explained by topological factors of closeness and enclosure.

The first problem of equilibration and regulation raised by the construction of representative space is to understand the "why" of this primacy of topological factors in terms of disturbances and compensations. We begin by studying the spatial representation as a part of the whole set of processes which characterize the conceptual assimilation at its beginning, i.e., as soon as the construction of the semiotic or symbolic function, based on the internalized imitation and the verbal signs, enables the subject to refer to absent objects (which naturally also modifies the assimilation of present objects). The arising representative assimilation consists essentially of using the conceptual schemes in "comprehension" and not in "extension" (cf. §20, the persistent difficulties of extension in the perception of collections of figures, etc.), in other words, in qualifying an object which is present by recognizing in it its various uses or consistency, color, form, etc., which make it possible to apply the scheme to it. In a general way, the disturbances are derived from the unforeseen qualities, differences, etc.,

---

[7] See J. Piaget and B. Inhelder, *La représentation de l'espace chez l'enfant*, Presses Universitaires de France.

[8] M. Laurendeau and A. Pinard, *Les premières notions spatiales de l'enfant*, Delachaux, 1968.

which require too great an accommodation, and compensation means separating the obstacles or integrating them insofar as it is possible. Which, then, are the characteristics of form specific to space but which can be replaced by the whole set of assimilating processes? They first intervene only within this mechanism. For an object to be assimilable, it must be consistent, continuous in time and space, isolatable, its parts must hold together, and it must be accessible to manipulation, etc. These are characteristics of a very general nature, which intervene before the subject is interested in form as such, and thus he must consider its spatial attributes independently of the others. It now becomes clear that the first forms retained will be those which qualify the object itself, independently of outside references, displacements, and perspectives, and those which furnish the best compensations for disturbing alterations of any kind. We can see that it is essential that the object forms a whole, is wrapped up in itself, and separated or separable from others but not dislocated as a whole, that its parts are close together, and above all that it possesses boundaries ensuring its closure and protecting its interior. It is surprising that in viewing the graphic representation of any form, even when the models presented are squares, triangles, etc., subjects strongly distinguish between closed and open forms, interior and exterior locations denoted by the boundaries, and retain only general characteristics of continuity, closure, and so forth, while neglecting angles, certain straight lines, and metric relations. Here is a compensation by cancellation of perceptual characteristics, and there is cancellation even after perception (the Euclidian figures are distinguished and recognized during choices involving perception). We will return (§22) to the methods of such omissions which are repressions of various degrees within which the assimilating schemes (here topological) play a compensating role.

2. The regulations leading from these topological schemes to Euclidian space are therefore very progressive. The first, which is still topological in nature, makes the

transition with the following levels and finally liberates the fundamental scheme of order from simple similarity. The order $ABCD$ . . . , the term B is close to both A and C, but C is no longer close to A, etc. When the young subject seeks to reproduce an ordered series of objects, we first see him committing errors due to the primacy of similarity, or closeness. For example, he tries DCB because C is close to D and like B, but corrects them because B would then not be close to A. After this, but following many corrections (which are therefore compensating regulations), he will know how to retain the order, or orientation, from the beginning to the end of the series instead of becoming the victim of inversions caused by the absence of directed neighboring composition.

These regulations producing order complete themselves by partitions resulting from the synthesis of closeness, separation, and returning. When the need is felt, separations are introduced within a content to distinguish and regulate the sectors. But this preoperational partition is by no means accompanied by a quantitative conservation of the whole.

Next the essential conquest of Euclidian space, itself a base for many others, is achieved, and we find the construction of the straight line for conservation of direction. The notion of direction is derived from that of order, since the latter is always orientated toward or away from a direction, and the regulations transforming the nearness into orders result, among other things, in maintaining one of these directions by opposing it to the other. Thus the direction applied to the segments of a unidimensional continuous line, or to a series of discrete but close and successive elements, at first produces just any line; e.g., when young subjects have to connect two points by a straight line, or more markedly when the points have discrete objects between them (for example, small trees along an indicated road), at first the subjects are satisfied with a wavy irregular line. The regulation which leads from this to the production of the straight line is seen, among developments, when the subject uses his two hands, placing them on either side of the line and verifying with greater and greater accuracy its straight characteristic. Actually the regulating corrections consist in compensating with a reverse modification any disturbance or deviation from the direction of the goal in order to preserve this direction from one end to another. In terms of partitions, and no longer of order, this means that any segment cut out of a straight line can be reinserted elsewhere without changing the line; however, if the end point coincides with the starting point (the two coincide), the line is circular.

If these constructions are all essentially compensating and at the same time productive, the very nature of the regulations present at their formation explains their limitations, i.e., the fact that the straight line is at first based simply on order and direction and that the length of the straight line is initially evaluated only as a function of its arrival point, that is, according to a partial boundary criterion. Thus in comparing a string and a bow, young subjects generally estimate them to be of the same length, since they have the same end points, although one is rectilinear and the other curvilinear. As for two parallel straight lines, the longest one is thought to be that which extends beyond the other without any consideration of departure points. When the subject considers only one of the directions, it is the arrival point that is important—at first nothing forces him to consider the opposite end (in general the regulations leading there only begin at the level of the reference systems).

The displacements also proceed from an ordinal construction, since they themselves are changes in order and are not "placements." They in turn include compensations which will later play a role in the structuring of the conservation of lengths and surfaces; a place left free is compensated as a new site of a displaced figure. In other words, in any displacement, the addition of space occupied at the end compensates the withdrawal of this space at the beginning. This is no play of words; we are dealing with very real compensations and the regulations they imply. There are two indications of this development. The first is that rather persistently in the subjects' preoperational representations (up to about the age of seven) perceptively empty space is not congruent with the full space.[9] Thus it is by regulations that the subject manages to compensate for the places left vacant and those which are newly occupied during displacements of figures on a background or solids in space; hence, he makes the empty and full spaces congruent (which is fundamental for the conservation of space). Second, these early regulations are followed by others which are similar and which, as we will see later, lead to conservations of lengths and surfaces.

3. We can study an example of these compensating regulations by using several objects to disrupt an initially blank surface. For equal surfaces, we used two cartons showing green meadows of grass grazed by cows. On one of these meadows we placed one house in a corner and another in the center: does the same green surface remain when the second house is added in the first meadow? On the second we placed the second house. Now do the green surfaces in the two meadows remain equal? In this experiment, the total unoccupied surface in each meadow was diminished by two equal amounts (the houses were naturally the same size. Thus we are again studying the perception of space but, in addition, we are questioning the formation of the Euclidian axiom according to which equal quantities subtracted from equal quantities leave equals.

This problem cannot usually be solved before the age of seven, and the regulations leading to its solution are often strikingly similar to the compensations mentioned previously. For example, a subject who first contests the equality of the remaining green spaces may move a house from its given position on the second meadow, place it in the same position as the corresponding one on the first meadow, and

---

[9] An empty space between two immobile objects is supposed to diminish in length if we place between them a large object such as a wall (except when the wall has a hole, which reestablishes the continuity of the empty space!).

then move it by stages back to its initial position, which makes him realize that the surface subtracted from each meadow is the same.

There are other examples of conservation of spatial size at this seven- to eight-year-old level. One experiment involves taking a segment out of a single strip and adding it to an end; after an initial stage the relationship between the extension and the transfer is comprehended. These developing conservations, whose formation requires the usual regulations and compensations, then allow the subject to free himself partially from ordering and to accede to abstract measurement. As we have shown above, this abstraction is based on a synthesis of partition and the ordering of displacements of a part which has been chosen as a unit, and it implies the transitivity of congruences obtained by these displacements. It would be useless to try to list the multiple regulations included in this complex construction which is entirely orientated, like the conservations it completes, in the compensation of numerous disturbances created by local alterations such as occur in any situation prior to the existence of invariants. In our understanding of space, measurement of objects is but a stage; the completion involves numbers on the terrain of discontinuous objects which are applied in three dimensions. Thus quantification will extend itself in a system of coordinates, and in this elaboration we will again find the most acute instances of compensations.

4. It is worth recalling the vast construction of projected space and the conceptualization of perspectives which run parallel to the preceding and with which it is synchronized. Here again, this conceptualization is something quite different from a perceptual process even though based on the constancy of the form. Because of the constancy of form, an object which is usually seen from perspective A conserves the same form even if it is seen from perspective B; i.e., in B it is perceived as if it were in A (by an immediate perceptual compensation, as we indicated in the preceding paragraph). To understand the conceptual comprehension, we must establish by which intermediary transformations

the object has passed from states A to B and, based on these transformations, determine in what form it will present itself if we displace it from B to a new position C (whether we alter distances, therefore apparent size, rotate the object, or in other ways change the retinal image).

The compensations summoned to vanquish the disturbances caused by these changes in position behave in a manner rather parallel to the one we described for displacements, except that the disturbances here are not involved solely with positions occupied by an invariant moving object but also with modifications of form and apparent size of an object as such. In fact, just as with displacements there are compensations between the spaces occupied and those left free, so when an object is turned, or the angle of vision is altered, the parts of the object which disappear from view or pass to the background are compensated by those which appear or move to the foreground; when the distance to objects is increased, the loss in apparent size of the objects is a function of its invariant dimensions. The situation is comparable to one in which operations of common direction are in play.

In studying the regulations themselves, we witness in the formative stages (before the age of seven or eight) a remarkable effort to anticipate disturbance, but we find compensations are only partially successful because of the inability to represent to oneself the transformation details. For example, when we say that we are going to show a flat watch not facing us but on its side, it is drawn as a half moon. The subject understands that part of the watch is going to disappear from the visual field, but as yet he does not see what will replace it and so simply does away with half the object that can be seen front view. A pencil, the tip of which we gradually raise until it is seen "standing," is drawn as if seen from the side (in such a manner that the drawing always retains the initial form), sometimes as merely diminished, but sometimes even as extended. We may assume either lack of differentiation between the displacement and the extension (see above), or compensation of what disappears by something new. It should be noted that the final position (the tip correctly seen as a small circle) is often seen before the closest intermediary positions, doubtless for the reason that the disappearance of part of the pencil may be compensated by another new one.

Moreover it should be noticed that in the problems of predicting surface from the unfolding of a cube, etc., the subject often reacts before the operational solutions are apparent by sketching the beginning of the results of the unfolding action (indicating a slight spread of one side, etc.). Here the accent is on the disturbances as transformations, but they are insufficiently understood to be integrated (see behaviors β and γ of §13), and likewise the compensation is insufficient to allow the subject to predict all the elements which until now were simultaneously invisible. The sketch will thus show at least a part of the still-folded section and one or two of the flattened elements.

An example from neither projective nor descriptive geometry is interesting, since it is related to changes of position. A square balanced on one of its corners is not considered by young children a square but a "double triangle" (diamond-shaped, etc.), since, according to the subjects, it is modified in its form and even in its dimensions. However, the compensation attempt makes them admit that while they see only a diamond shape, the experimenter, if he faces a side of the figure, clearly sees a square. The displacement of the square is then compensated by the opposite displacement of the subject who perceives it.

5. At the nine- to ten-year-old level the representation of space shows two kinds of achievements: first, the generalization of three-dimensional quantified space leads to a general system of references or natural orthogonal coordinates, and second, the subject manages to perceive changes due to perspective for several objects at once (a whole set of three carton assemblies seen from the four cardinal points, etc.). We must now show that these new constructions are themselves animated by compensating processes.

To study coordinates, let us begin with a situation that raises the question of references outside figures. When one of two rods, which has been proved equal in length to the other by congruence, is pushed so that it extends by about half its size beyond the other, children up to the age of nine generally consider this movement as an extension and a transfer, both undifferentiated; i.e., the rod that is pushed ahead is believed to have become longer than the other. It is obvious then that the regulations, preceding the deductive operation that ensures conservation, will sooner or later (but with numerous oscillations) modify the compensations between what the displaced rod gains in the forward direction and what it loses behind (cf. the interpretation of displacements).

But in such an example, it is recourse to outside references which makes it possible to prove equality of rod segments and spaces left empty by displacements. Without this it would be necessary to use a measuring device which the subject will not consider before suggesting the compensation or before supposing that, relative to the table acting as a support, the rod will be the same length before and after the displacement.

In addition to the system of coordinates arising from the generalization of measures in two or three dimensions, there are immobile references and their compensations which are similar to those just discussed. Let us consider two immobile references, A and B, and between the two a moving object which passes from the one to the other. The distance between A and this moving object is a, and that which extends between the moving object and B is a'. It is evident that if the sum $a + a'$ is judged to be a constant, any decrease in a' is compensated by an increase in a. Now, the difficulty subjects up to about the age of nine have in comprehending the equality of front and rear displacement when a rod is moved ahead of a rod of equal length, and especially in connecting the movement of the rod and its extension (except when the rod is seen as a measuring unit against an immobile object which then plays the role of the object measured and not of reference), shows that the evidence of this compensation between a' and a is not immediate, and therefore the compensation requires regulations which intervene in the construction of the reference systems.

These references are particularly delicate and therefore easy to observe in the following two situations. The first development takes place during the same period as the formation of systems of coordinates and is equivalent. We can follow from the fourth or fifth year up to the ninth or tenth the acquisition of perspective coordinations and the role of the compensations. After much groping, the subject can coordinate the effects of perspective changes on a whole set of objects, for example, three mountains which, according to the vantage point, pass from the foreground to the background or vice versa, and from right to left or vice versa.

The second development, evident at eleven or twelve, is the response to the necessity to coordinate two systems of reference at the same time, one of which is mobile and the other immobile. An object's displacements on the mobile system is capable of being compensated by movements in the opposite direction of the mobile system itself, while the position in relation to the immobile system remains unchanged. In this case, two kinds of compensations intervene: one by inversion (when it is the same object or system which displaces itself in one direction or another), the other by reciprocity (occurring between two distinct entities); therefore, the necessity of three entities which are coordinated by these two operations.

On the whole, it seems clear that from the formation of the initial topological structures up to superior behaviors, any spatial construction, however striking its novelty as compared to those of the preceding levels, is based on a compensation because each new solution arises on the occasion of a disturbance of the schemes of the preceding level. Moreover these disturbances and their compensations closely follow the order of the behaviors described in §13. Compensations occur through modification of opposites or cancellations at the lower levels, then through gradual integrations of the disturbances, which become variations in the system, and finally through symmetries so that these variations and their opposites are promoted to the rank of operations proper. Now, one of the fundamental aspects of this development of behaviors from type α to type γ is the internalization of negations, at first imposed from without, then integrated in the form of degrees of variations (in the form of "more or less"), and finally in the form of inverse operations characteristic of the operational structures. This role of negations and affirmations is even clearer in the compensations in play during the construction of exclusively logico-mathematical structures (the space here, as before, participates in the geometry of the objects), and this is what we are now going to study.

Four

THE
LOGICO-MATHEMATICAL
STRUCTURES

§19/ *The Conservation of Quantities*

The concept of equilibration in the development of notions of conservation creates complex problems treated rather summarily in our essay *Logique et équilibre*, 1957, as though it were dependent on the probabilities of encounter between the subject and the object's characteristics, whereas we see compensating regulations intervene, which lead to the correspondence of the positive and negative aspects of transformations.

1. Let us recall the ball of clay extended into a sausage shape, and list the levels observed which we will express in terms of observables and inferential coordinations.

Level I. Nonconservation: the subject generally concentrates only on the length of the sausage. We then have *Obs. S* = the action of extension in a single direction. Hence the *Obs. O* = the increase in length without consideration of other dimensions.

Coord. S and *Coord. O* concern the increase of the quantity which as yet can be evaluated only in an ordinal manner by comparison of initial and final states, and the action itself which is seen as merely producing a qualitative change of state (in opposition to continuous transformations).

Level II (transition). The *Obs. S* remain centered on the drawing-out but it is progressive (in a more or less continuous manner), and sooner or later leads the subject by observation of contrast to discover two kinds of *Obs O*: extension and thinning.

The inferential *Coord. S* and *Coord. O* then remain in unstable equilibrium; i.e., there is an increase of quantity as long as centration is on the extension and decrease of substance when the thinning is noticed.

Level III. The *Obs. S* and the *Obs. O* are differentiated and integrated as the drawing-out action becomes distinct from, and bound up with, the thinning. In our research with Inhelder on the mental image, we thus found at about the age of six an intermediary level where the students, without achieving conservation, managed to see correctly that in stretching out the sausage they are making it "long and thin" (cf. the case of Bel, 6; 1, page 326).[1] It is evident therefore that this novelty concerns the *Obs. O* as much as the *Obs. S*. It even seems very probable that the idea of a unit between the drawing-out by the subject and the thinning of the sausage can be established only as a function of the results observed on the object, since nothing forces the subject who stretches it to be aware of the fact that he is thinning it also; i.e., the pulling action is not differentiated from the mere tactile-kinesthetic viewpoint in successive moments, nor even perceived in two distinct dimensions if attention is not centered in advance on this possibility. Thus it is very probable that the *Obs. O* of the thinning (occasionally noticed at the transition level II) act as a return on the *Obs. S*.

---

[1] J. Piaget and B. Inhelder, *L'image mentale chez l'enfant*, Paris, Presses Universitaires de France.

This correlation of the *Obs. O* and *Obs. S* then produces *Coord. S* and *Coord. O* which, on level IV, result in the conservation. What is new, as compared to level II, is that the extension and thinning are no longer conceived as successive or alternating modifications with no relation between them, but rather as solidly connected effects coming simultaneously from the same action. Moreover, and partly because of this connection, this action is no longer one way. Without consciously considering reversibility, the subjects often by themselves anticipate a possible return to the original state (reversibility without conservation during two changes). On the other hand, what level III still lacks is the comprehension of the fact that this connection between an increase and a decrease expresses a quantitative compensation; the concept is limited to two qualitative variations with distinct directions, but they do not cancel each other. Nevertheless, the progress gained from the connection of the qualitative changes is marked by the displacement of the effect of the *Coord. S* and *Coord. O*. The subject no longer limits himself to a static comparison between the initial and final stage, with false inferences of nonconservation, but begins to comprehend the change as such, since it may even appear double or bipolar. In addition, the inferential intuition of a reversibility of some of the action reinforces this nascent perception of the characteristic of transformation and even enables the subject, aware of weak variations, to glimpse a possible conservation although there is still no justification.

Level IV. Here the remarkable fact is that the extension and thinning are at once as effects of the stretching action. ("It will be longer then, not thick," a subject says.) This implies that the *Coord. S* and *Coord. O* of the preceding level (leading to the unity between the two transformations) have modified these observables by introducing between them the beginnings of a necessary connection, without which the subject could only make a simple inductive generalization with the uncertainties it includes. The proof that this inferred need is answered at this level is that the two transformations of extension and thinning (or, with the change of a ball into a round slab, of increase in diameter and flattening) are immediately conceived (implicitly or explicitly) as compensating each other quantitatively, although the subject makes no measure at all nor shows the slightest interest in empirical verification. It is this characteristic of inferred necessity (and valid necessity) of the *Coord. S* and *Coord. O*, largely extending beyond the boundaries of the observables, which leads to the perception of the conservation of the quantity of matter, although as yet there is no conception of conservation of weight or volume. The conservation of matter thus appears to be of observable significance.

2. The whole construction of the conservation, evident in levels I through IV, is dominated by a general process. After reacting only with static comparisons between the initial and final stage, the subject begins to make inferences dealing with the transformations as such and to make relational evaluations. It is evident, therefore, that this passage from static states to transformation with conservation is the work of regulations whose feedback forces retroactions which displace the centrations of thought to the continuous modifications of the object.

We can distinguish three characteristics of their final forms which will then enable us to isolate their mechanism. The first of these achievements we can call "commutability," and it enables the subject to understand that what increases one dimension of an object—for example, the length of a sausage—necessarily corresponds to what is removed from another. At the start, the subject, centered on the result of the stretching action, merely considers the final increase without bothering about the attendant subtraction, which is an experimental finding in conformity with the general law (reason for nonbalance at the beginning) of the initial primacy of positive elements over the negations. With commutability, however, this kind of creation ex nihilo, which the subject implicitly refers to when perceiving an increase of the total quantity, is altered so that there is perception of a mere displacement of part of the object and the identification of what is displaced (i.e., a part is removed from one point and added elsewhere); hence, there is a kind of generalized commutativity—conservation of the sum of parts despite their change in position. This is what the subject expresses by means of the first argument which we always obtain as justification of the conservation: "Nothing has been removed or added; we just stretched it." There is no comment such as "It is the same quantity of clay."

The second result of the regulations is a form of rearrangement. A category B can be subdivided into a starting category, A_1, and its complement, A'_1. But we can also begin at any level with another subcategory, A_2, whose complement under B will be A'_2. We then have $A_1 + A'_1 = A_2 + A'_2 = B$, although A_1 is part of A'_2 and A of A'_1. The comprehension of the rearrangement means understanding that whatever the divisions, and independently of their spatial arrangements, we find the same whole. The difference between rearrangement and mutability is that the latter is centered on the identity of the displaced parts (and those resting in place) and determines from the evidence the invariance of their sum, whereas rearrangement denotes the constancy of the sum, whatever partitions are made and whatever the spatial arrangement. We can therefore say that commutability involves rearrangement and vice versa; and, when the child uses what is generally his second argument, "We can make the ball again out of the sausage, therefore it's the same size," this insight into reversibility can be based on the concept of rearrangement as well as on commutability. The difference between this reasoning and the simple empirical return to the original form, but without conservation, is that it states the equivalence regarding the whole, B, no matter what the forms (or divisions of parts), e.g., whether changing from the sausage to the ball or from the ball to the sausage. But it should be noted that the rearrangement also includes partial negations, for any part plays its operational role in the composition; i.e., it is conceived as being "equal to the whole less the other parts" ($A_1 = B - A'_1$, etc.) Otherwise the whole would vary in size according to the arrangement of the parts (which is frequent in the nonconservations of surfaces, etc.).

The third result of the regulations (and it is used as the third argument by the child) is the well-known compensation of variations; e.g., when the length increases, the diameter of the sausage decreases, etc.

Let us note, furthermore, that if the commutability and the rearrangement imply in their finished form of reasoning in "extension" (referring to the sum of the categories or of subcategories or, in infralogical form, of parts) the compensation of regulations, involving "more or less," they remain dependent on the "comprehension" and on a simple serial correspondence between increasing lengths and decreasing diameters which result in "correlates" in the Spearman sense. In fact, we are fully aware that this compensation of relations occurs earlier than any measuring or quantification other than that inherent in ordinal or serial relations. This is of some interest, as one can see the beginnings of this compensation at level III.

3. We are not dealing with a regulation of actions concerned with a physical goal, for the transformation of a small ball into a sausage presents no difficulty and can be achieved at any age. The regulations deal only with perceiving observables and inferential coordinations; therefore, the sole disturbances in play result from contradictions or nonbalance between the observables or inferences imposed by the facts on the nascent coordinations. At the start (level I) there is no problem; the child proceeds to stretch the ball and concludes that there is an increase of quantity without noticing the decrease of diameter. Thus he experiences a kind of creation of matter. The first disturbance arises between these *Obs. O* and a new *Obs. S* when he realizes this extension is really accomplished by successive stretches, which tends to substitute the notion of a displacement for that of absolute increase. But since at these levels the dis-

placement of a moving object does not exclude its extension, the inference (retrospective or anticipatory) concerns an increase in quantity. A more serious disturbance is then produced by the new *Obs. O* which suggest that the sausage thins while being stretched out. What the corrections or conceptual regulations then must coordinate are the two facts of an increase in length resulting from the displacement of the clay and the thinning of the sausage. It is this double requirement which later leads to making the added (+) parts at the far end of the sausage correspond to what is "removed" (−) from the initial ball; i.e., increases in length (+) must correspond to decreases in diameter (−).

These progressive compensations, regulating but incomplete before becoming operational and whole, result at level IV in commutability or rearrangement and in reversible correspondences of relations. We now need to determine if the compensations for the alterations expressed in the positive and negative features just discussed finally complete themselves using the commutability process or that of rearrangement; the first achieving the conservation of the whole from the identification of the parts, at both the points from which they are removed and the locations to which they are taken, and the second based on the fact that divisions or alterations of form do not change but conserve the size of the sum of the complementary parts. Actually, in the special case where the rearrangement is not static (different division of subsystems without displacements in space) but involves changes in spatial relations, the two methods complete each other; the one beginning with the conservation of elements during their displacements, and the other with the reunion of the parts. Negations are handled in a similar way: the consistent commutability enables the subtraction at the start to be balanced by the addition at the end, whereas the concept of rearrangement allows the negation to express the relation between one part and the others as parts of a whole. From such a viewpoint the two procedures are equally necessary.

In addition, we may consider the positive and negative

characteristics of the forms of the whole object. The parts of areas displaced by a stretching action naturally are not discontinuous, and when the subject manages to understand the compensation between what he removes from one area and adds to another, he is considering not only those sections pushed or drawn by the fingers, but changes in a continuous whole. Thus these displacements are recognized as modifying the form of the whole, and the thinning is correlated with the extension, so that these changes lead to the conclusion that the additions compensate the losses. After noticing in a sporadic and unstable manner the sausage's thinning, the subject arrives at level III and understands the constant unity between the extension and thinning. It is then that this "comprehension" of unity (by inverse serial correspondence between positive and negative variations) becomes the necessary complement of, if not the reason for, the perception of compensation.

Although the displaced parts are not isolable nor the variations in form measurable, the general problem is to understand the final situation to which these various compensations in the subject's mind lead. On the one hand, inferential necessity indicates the closing of an operational structure, and on the other, conservation of the whole is the common characteristic of "groupings" whose essential operations include identity $(= O)$ and the inverse function[2] $(T \cdot T^{-1} = 1$, that is, the complete compensation of negations and affirmations. If the preceding is correct, commutability, rearrangements, and compensations of relations in additions and losses—three expressions or derivatives of groupings—do not constitute the first facts but rather are the results of the regulating methods. It is striking to note how the mechanism of disturbances creating regulations—in our example we see the discovery of the sausage's thinning out—evolves during the three stages described in §13. At level I there is a kind of repression of the observable although it is quite perceptible, which is a type α behavior. After fluctuations

---

[2] Let us recall that if T is a direct operation T^{-1} is its opposite.

at level II, the thinning becomes, at level III, bound up with the stretching out, and thus no longer constitutes a disturbance but a variation integrated in the system. This is the result of a type β behavior. Finally, at level IV, this variation becomes by deduction essential for the whole system, and with its inverse operations (type γ behavior) ensures an exact correspondence between the negations and the affirmations. But this level is attained only after a long equilibration by regulations whose reversibility is a result and not the driving force of the accomplishments.

§20/   *The Classification and Quantification of the Inclusion*

In an interpretation of equilibration where the reason for the initial nonbalance is attributed to the sustained primacy of affirmations, or of positive elements in the cognitive systems and the lack of correlated negations, although progressive equilibrium requires symmetry and necessary correspondences, it is useful to return to questions of classification and the difficulties of determining what is included. If all the problems of classification are reduced to questions of coordination between similarities and differences, it is still clear that differences consist in virtual negations or at least imply them. It is therefore interesting to see if the regulations and the progressive compensations which they tend to establish are going to be centered on the construction of negations, and if so, what successive forms they will take.

1. Let us begin by recalling the four principal levels in the development of classifications:[3]

Level I. Given instructions such as "Put together what is

---

[3] In *La genèse des structures logiques élémentaires*, Inhelder and Piaget distinguish only three principal levels, the present level II there being presented only as the beginning of the great stage here known as III.

similar," the child begins by choosing an object and then locates another similar object and places it alongside the first. Then, proceeding faster and faster without any anticipatory scheme and by juxtaposition, he succeeds in changing criteria (for example, he shifts from form to color) or in giving them up for new kinds of agreement (for example, a triangle is placed on a square as though he were building a house). The result is a collection which presents a definite spatial form, i.e., alignments, columns, two-dimensional figures (rectangles, etc.). We will speak of this as a "figural collection." It is the result of two processes: "comprehension" due to broader and broader assimilations, and "extension" which, for lack of anticipation of the variety of the elements in the collection, confers on the collection a progressively elaborated geometrical form. We recognize in these reactions a level analogous to the first in the development of seriation during which the elements are not yet arranged by size but merely juxtaposed, e.g., small sticks aligned in more or less parallel fashion but without regard for size.

Level II. This transition level is not well defined but marks the beginning of what will be stage III. (Here are nonfigural and hierarchized collections which correspond to the complete but empirical seriation of § 21.) The organization at this level corresponds to the uncoordinated pairs and trios which characterize the second seriation level; there is no serial structure for the whole, so there is only juxtaposition of small elementary series. The lower forms belonging to this level consist of figural collections but later they show superimposed alignments (or obliques and parallels, etc.), each of which includes analogous elements that are distinct from those of other subcollections. The superior forms are small, nonfigural, but juxtaposed collections without unique criterion, and there may or may not be a heterogeneous residue. An intermediary form between levels II and III achieves the use of a unique criterion for classification (color, form, etc.) but still without hierarchies.

Level III. The subject at once constructs nonfigural collections, this time with subdivisions of these collections and subcollections, and this nascent hierarchy can give the impression of an operational classification, as the empirical seriations of level III can refer to completed seriations. But just as the type III seriations are not yet accompanied by transitivity, so the subjects at this same stage do not succeed in quantifying the inclusions. And, for a category B such that $B = A + A'$, they do not succeed in realizing that there are necessarily more individual elements in B than in A; in fact, if B is subdivided into A and A', the subcategory A is compared by them only to A' and no longer to any unattached B.

Level IV. The classification is now and henceforth formed of properly logical categories subdivided into subcategories and is accompanied by quantification of inclusions. It is also possible consciously to shift criteria and construct multiple systems (double entry tables, etc.).

2. The interest in the first of these levels lies in the fact that the subject looks exclusively for resemblances and neglects any differences. What we see is identical with the instructions given the subjects: "Put together what is similar," etc. But it is clear, and the spontaneous reactions at the consequent levels reveal this quite well, that such directions logically imply "Do not place together what is not similar." However, the subject sticks to a single collection and for each new element manages to find a positive relation with the preceding one, no longer concerning himself with the previous criterion. Here a second factor intervenes: the incapacity of anticipating the collection in its extension because now the collection will be determined by certain qualities common to all its elements, which at the same time will suggest the elimination of those lacking these characteristics. The subject succeeds by attributing at the very outset, or during the process, a form of the whole to the objects, which is again based solely on similarities but applies to the spatial whole and no longer concerns the elements as "parts" (in the infralogical or "mereological" sense) of this continuous whole nor as discrete parts of a category. Since

assimilation is the basic factor in this elaboration of concepts (as it was in sensorimotor schemes), we can consider the differences between elements as disturbances which are cancelled or neglected at this level (level I) in conformity with type a behavior.

But these disturbances begin to have an effect at level II. Here the compensating regulation reinforces the similarities, and all the elements are no longer placed in the same totality (which actually means respecting the similarities only between an element and its immediate predecessor(s) or conferring an overall significance on the whole), but actually analogous objects are made to form small collections and these are located in separate regions. Thus these solutions achieve an equilibrium between the similarities and the differences, since these small collections are composed of elements at once similar to one another yet different from those which are situated in other collections. But what is lacking is a total category which would include these collections as subcategories with their special characteristics subordinated to the common qualities.

3. At level III the equilibrium of similarities and differences is attained, because the regulations leading from II to III compensate the remaining differences between the small collections and liberate the common characteristics which are capable of gathering all the collections into a total category. The nonfigural and hierarchized collections resulting from this partial equilibrium then give, as we have already said, a false impression of operational classification, because here only similarities and differences are considered and differences can always be conceived and formulated under the auspices of affirmative judgments; i.e., what these systems lack is the abstraction of negations, and we can even say that at this level negations are not included. In fact, given a subcategory A included in B, the subject at level III clearly sees that if all the A are B, there exists a subcategory of A' which are also B but which are "different" from A. He will no doubt tell us that the A' are therefore not A, but his comprehension remains verbal, and on the opera-

tional level he understands so little of the relations between categories and subcategories ($B = A + A'$ where $A =$ the B not A' and $A' =$ the B not A) that he cannot free the evidence according to which there are necessarily more elements in the category of the whole, B, than in the subcategory A. In other words, for lack of negation and of the inverse operation, which is subtraction, he does not succeed in quantifying the inclusions. When he is asked to compare A and B he limits himself to a comparison of A and A', as if the difference between the whole and the parts were the same as the difference between the parts, or as though a whole, here B, once subdivided into parts no longer existed as a totality but was reduced to what remained, A', once the part removed, A, was set aside.

This difficulty in quantifying the inclusion in the form of $B > A$ is clearly due to a problem with negation and not with enumeration, since a numerical comparison of A and B is easy by correspondence. For the subject, the central problem is to understand that if the whole, B, and the part, A, are both different and alike, the similarity wins out in the affirmative form "all the A are B," whereas the difference should be expressed in the negative form "all the B are not A," indicating $B > A$. It is for lack of this insight that a child at this level comes to grief. Let us mention here the attractive counterproof designed by Inhelder, Sinclair, and Bovet and reported in their *Apprentissage et structures de la connaissance*. For example, they asked subjects to increase the numerical value of the subcategory A and leave B constant. At level III the subjects either add the same number of elements to A and A' (hence increase B, contrary to directions), or they are clever enough to do away with A' and increase A; with both responses they avoid a subtraction from A'. Only the subjects at operational level IV realize that they must decrease A' by n and add n to A, thereby admitting that for a given whole an addition to A implies a subtraction from A' and vice versa.

Finally, at level IV, the differences and similarities are balanced completely as the differences are understood as partial negations; i.e., A' becomes B *not* A and A becomes B *not* A'. This evolution exhibited in levels I through IV, which lasts from about three to eight years of age, thus shows in the clearest manner how the increasing equilibration is composed of a gradual development of compensations of positive characteristics and negations. Let us repeat: the initial nonbalance is due to the primacy of similarities, while disturbances, represented in this situation by the differences, are usually ignored (type α behavior). Later the disturbing negations are integrated in the system (type β behavior) but in the restricted form of simple differences without their being recognized as authentic inverse operations. Finally, at the last level (type γ behavior), the differences lead to partial negations ($A' = B - A$), and the subject understands the strict relation between direct and inverse operations.

§21/ *Seriation and Transitivity*

The development of serial order, although treated far more often than classification or inclusions, nevertheless requires a review in the light of our understanding of equilibration, first, because it was insufficiently analyzed in our earlier work on the cognitive equilibrium, and second, because we have treated the compensation of the positive characteristics and negations, dominating the whole problem of increasing equilibration, in a very specific manner. In its use of equilibration seriation is completely different from classification. In classification similarities and differences form opposite categories; in seriation greater or smaller resemblances are equivalent to greater or smaller differences.

1. First, let us recall the following five levels (using the problem of the seriation of ten elements).

Level I. Rulers are arranged in a vertical more or less parallel manner without regard to size.

Level IIA and IIB. The subject succeeds in constructing juxtaposed pairs, consisting in each case of a small and a large element, such as $D < F$, or $A < H$, etc., but there are no interpair connections. In IIB he proceeds in the same way by forming trios (a "small," a "middle," and a "large" size) but does not order the trios.

Level II–III (transition). The subject succeeds in obtaining a staircase pattern for the tops of the rulers but does not bother with the bases. Or he constructs a figure in the form of a roof (a rise then fall of a line over the tops) with the bases now forming an even horizontal line. Or at best, finally, he succeeds in seriating four or five elements but remains blocked for the rest.

Let us note that at the outset of this transition level, the subject is often capable of drawing in advance (fifty-five percent of the subjects at the age of five) the series as he was asked to construct them, although he cannot complete the construction. Let us mention also that a subject drawing ten elements already seriated is seen to experience stages I–III, and has the ability to make corrections as early as the age of five.

Level III. The entire series is finally ordered but by an empirical groping method, that is, with local errors and corrections afterward. On the other hand, the subject has not yet mastered the transitivity problem; if we show him $X < Y$, and $Y < Z$ (while hiding X), he does not conclude that necessarily $X < Z$. In addition, once the ten initial elements are ordered, if we give the subject one or two additional rulers to insert, he does not succeed at once and prefers to begin the entire construction again with all the old and new elements. Also, if the experimenter gives the subject ten unordered elements and asks him to give them back, one by one, in the serial order, or to place them successively in this order behind a screen, the subject cannot perform the task.

Level IV. The transitivity is understood, and two additional tasks can be successfully completed. The subject generally begins with (or soon learns to use) a method, both systematic and exhaustive, which consists first in seeking the smallest element, then the smallest of those remaining, etc.

This process implies the comprehension of the fact that any element E is both greater than the preceding $(E > D, C, B, A)$, and smaller than the following $(E < F, G,$ etc.$)$; thus the ability to utilize both reversibility $(>$ and $<)$ and transitivity.

2. Level I is interesting in that, as with classifications, the subject at the start neglects differences, and this happens despite the instructions which specifically request finding gradations from the smallest to the largest. At the outset of level II, the difference is accepted, but here again, as with the classifications, in a form not incorporating any negation; an element expresses only positive characteristics and is either "small" or "large." This means the relations "more" and "less" are ignored, with the consequence that one element cannot be part of two differences at the same time. When the ten small rulers are regarded as a single category, it can only be divided into two subcategories, one of all the small rulers and one of all the large rulers. When each element is considered individually, it can be put in a relationship with any other, although not simultaneously related to two. The subject may understand that $B > A$ and also that $B < C$, but on the transition level II–III, when the relations $>$ and $<$ appear together, the subject will feel they are incompatible. Consequently, he can only arrange the rulers by pairs (one small and one large) and show no relations between the pairs, since this would imply double comparisons.

Once these various pairs are juxtaposed, the disturbance which then intervenes is caused by the resulting disorder. The unordered sizes of the pairs are perceptively quite distinct, so the correction consists in recognizing a new difference. The "means" for the correction then belongs neither to the small nor to the large but to a third category,[4] as

---

[4] In 1957 we wrongly thought that they formed a beginning of connections between the relations $<$ and $>$, but studies made since by Sinclair on the memory of seriations and their linguistic expression show the characteristic still predicative and prerelative of the "means."

squares added to circles and triangles would demand a new category.

The progress then involves a division of the whole into three categories—small, medium, and large—or a juxtaposition of trios not coordinated among themselves. It should be noted, however, that the order required by the instruction begins to be realized as is indicated by the trios which are seriated internally in a regular manner (small, medium, large), but which remain as isolated perceptions, since there is no physical ordering of the trios.

3. The disorder which remains thus gives rise to compensation tests; compromises which make a transition with level III and result either in constructing a staircase to fit a preconceived summit line, while neglecting positions of the bases of the rulers, or in changing the trios into series of four or five elements. We then witness, in the realm of relations in "comprehension," the formation of interesting "prerelations" which Sinclair named "labeling" and which are similar to the predicative judgments "very small," "rather small," "small average," "average," "large," etc.

The corrections and regulations included in this elaboration are at their zenith at level III, and it is now that the construction of the series is completed, but it is empirically built by groping and after much temporary error. From our present viewpoint, this is the most significant stage, for if these tests really result in the synthesis of similarities and differences which are essential for a regular seriation, there is as yet no comprehension of the compensation of positive characteristics and negations, in other words, of the necessary relation of "more" and "less." Certainly, while making his local corrections, the subject is led to consider alternatively relations of "greater than" and "less than," which render partially relative the predicates "small," "medium," and "large"; but the constructed series continues to be viewed as having a single direction and the subject still does not recognize the double characteristic of a difference which indicates both "larger" (than the preceding) and "smaller" (than the following). As Sinclair showed, when we ask a subject to describe the finished series as it "works" in the two directions, he is hindered; for example, the next to last element is "even larger" in the ascending sense, but "smaller" in the descending sense. However, the comparative terms "larger" and "smaller" are already acquired.

On the other hand, recent research with Liambey and Papandropoulou revealed that, up to the age of about seven, the subjects note that n elements are larger than the first and still cannot conclude that there are as many smaller than the last.

4. Finally, at level IV, the preceding regulations achieve the state of reversible operations, which signifies that the similarities and differences are now related in positive and negative terms which are quantitative; i.e., the "more" and the "less" exactly compensate each other. This compensation, finally completed, is recognized as an extension to equality or manifest as "greater than" and "less than" in seriations, or as "smaller" and "larger" attributes allowing for inverse operations. But it is chiefly recognized by two novelties. The first is that construction of the series can proceed without groping, and as we have seen (under section 1) by combination of $E > D, C, B, A$ and of $E < F, G$, or again we see immediate intercalation of elements added after the series is formed. The second, of great importance, is the ability to use transitivity. This relation results directly from the mechanisms of compensation of $(+)$ and $(-)$, for if $(+) + (-) = O$, then $(+) + (+) = (++)$ and $(-) + (-) = (=--)$. Hence $(A < B) + (B < C) = A << C$ where the symbol $<<$ expresses the reunion of the two given relations $<$ and $<$. In fact, these formative mechanisms are those of a reversible composition, hence the return of C to A, but this is simply another manner of expressing the compensation of $(+)$ and $(-)$, for if we call a the relation $(A < B)$, and a' the relation $(B < C)$, we have $a + a' = b$ and $b - a'' = a$.

On the whole, the entire evolution of the seriation is dominated by two kinds of progressive compensations arising from the initial nonbalance: one between the similarities and the differences, and the other between the positive characteristics and their negations. At level I, the differences are not retained nor the increases and the decreases related by a double elimination of disturbing factors (type a behaviors). At levels II and III there is an integration of the differences (type a behaviors), but there are as yet no relations between the increases and the decreases. At level IV what was disturbing is entirely internalized and integrated in the form of direct and inverse operations (type β behaviors). Thus there is comprehension of equivalences between sizes more or less different and less or more similar, and of the possible composition of these relations, hence of transitivity.

Thus, it seems justified to consider this gradual equilibration between the disturbances (progressively internalized) and the compensating reactions as not being deducible analytically from the characteristics of the final stage. This stage thus constitutes the psychogenetic product of a formative process which does not contain in advance the terminal operations but only a very general method of compensating reactions for disturbances arising from the simplest, and consequently the most probable, but not the most logical, actions. Here the operational logic appears once again as the unpremeditated result (by abstraction of time-space and dynamic factors) of a temporary psychological equilibration, and not as its source.

III

General Questions

Five

THE EQUILIBRATION
OF OBSERVABLES
AND COORDINATIONS

§22/ *The Regulations Concerning the Observables
on the Object* (Obs. O)

An observable in the sense in which we have taken this term
concerning interactions of types I and II (§9 to 12) is a
verifiable fact. Now, everyone admits (and "logical positivism" was forced to recognize it when the Vienna Circle[1]
stuck to the *Protokollsätze* based solely on perception) that
a fact goes beyond the perceptive datum and always includes, from the very moment it is recognized, a conceptualization determining the direction of the interpretation. That is why we have admitted that our observables

---

[1] A group of logicians studying the logic of science in the belief
that such a logic would provide a unified science. The physicalism
and scientific empiricism are among the tenets which strongly influence psychology.——*Trans.*

were all conceptualized at the appropriate levels, which is evident for those concerning the objects (*Obs. O*), but is no less true for those dealing with the action proper (*Obs. S*), for the awareness of them also constitutes a conceptualization.

1. Nevertheless any observable includes, as the substance or content of this conceptualization, a certain perceptual fact (in its largest meaning which is, for the action proper, above all of a proprioceptive nature) although it can be well or poorly observed. Yet we have seen that the perceptual regulations depend on purely perceptual mechanisms only in limited cases (for example, centration with slight distortions compensated by other centrations, etc.) and that in the situations which interest us here, it is the conceptualization that guides and orientates the perceptual activities in the directon of the most important corrections. In the following discussion we will not return to the truly perceptual regulations and will limit ourselves to the problems concerning only the conceptualized verification. Part Three is devoted to a study of these problems through the analysis of compensating regulations intervening in the elaboration of observables and in the construction of coordinations.

In utilizing observables (in contrast to the inferential coordinations, *Coord. S* and *Coord. O*) subjects can make constructions of two kinds: first, the conceptualization itself of each observable, and second the patterning of relations of observables, especially the *Obs. O* and *Obs. S* or the *Obs. Y* and *Obs. X* (§10 through 12). At first glance these constructions appear modest. But it is clear that the conceptualization will depend, virtually from the outset, on the patterning of relations. Next it should be noted that this patterning of relations which begins with mere comparisons can include the dependent functions which also depend on the verifications, hence on the observables. This is true of the empirical laws in general (contrary to the causal explanations which go beyond them). In addition, it is obvious that these conceptualizations, especially this patterning of relations, include the use of preoperational or operational instruments, invented on the occasion of the presentation of facts, or applied to them in the form of new morphisms. We can feel confident, therefore, that the term "construction" is by no means exaggerated when used to designate the totality; and hence the problem of compensations is posed in the most natural manner, since such constructions are constantly threatened by contradictions (between the perceived contents and the conceptual forms, between the conceptual forms derived from one observable and another, between observables and the constructed relations required to unite them, etc.) and contradictions between facts or notions always denote incomplete compensations.

Thus let us now attempt to describe, in terms of observables, the relations between constructions and compensations by distinguishing the different varieties of regulations and attempt to specify the functions each assumes.

2. The elementary regulations are those which for a given observable adjust a conceptual form to its perceptual content. Here we would have to distinguish two cases: that in which the perceptual content is related to an outside object and that in which it is related to the action proper, so that the conceptual form is part of the conceptualization or "awareness." The first case is simpler. Let us begin with it and recall two previous remarks. First, we must remember that this regulation by adjustment of a form to a content is special to thought, hence to cognitive structures based on a semiotic function, and does not exist at the sensorimotor levels where the scheme is not as yet the equivalent of a concept. In fact, a sensorimotor action implies or includes perceptual elements as much as motivation and does not depend on a distinction between form and content but on the repetitions and generalizations which liberate the scheme. But if the action thus simplified, i.e., generalized, is applied to new objects, it is not through a conceptual form which adjusts itself to the content, since the object is definitely not modified in sensorimotor situations except by enrichment of form, whereas at the higher levels it is changed materially. Second, let us repeat that the form-

content regulation—we will give examples of this—corresponds to relation *a* in the model of interactions IB (§9), that is, it is found at the junction between the subject's activity, *As*, and the object's resistance, real or not. However, in discussing model IB we spoke of type *a* relations in situations in which subjects applied whole structures (classifications, etc.) to whole sets of objects, whereas here we will use type *a* relations in describing the conceptualization of isolated observables.

The regulation we will now study actually intervenes in all situations where the subject confers on observables qualities only partially corresponding to their perceivable characteristics, either because one of these predicate qualities is erroneously applied or because the characteristics originally perceived remain incomplete. It goes without saying that the initial conceptualizations are almost always insufficient because of one or another of these two problems. Therefore we must reestablish according to which regulating mechanism readjustment of the conceptual form to the perceptual content is made. Such a problem can appear nonexistent or trivial, since during the experiencing the subject limits himself to recording the object's characteristics, or if in a sequential manner, simultaneously, without making readjustments. If we consider the assimilations, however, we must explain why the subject begins by forming an exact, distorted, or even incomplete conception of the object, and we face a real problem in trying to understand which regulations will produce an equilibrium between the assimilating forms and the content to which they accommodate themselves.

When a quality given to an object is illusory and distorting, we can say that this false *Obs. O* is due to coordinations which are themselves erroneous or incomplete. For example, the motion attributed to immobile mediators under the influence of an internal motion may be conceived of as external or semiexternal. But distortion may also be due to an omission, that is, to observables insufficiently analyzed; for example, the constant width which a child attributes to a sausage during its extension (see §19) when he neglects its thinning (as in our experiments on conservation). In general the simple conceptualizations of the observables involve no apparent distortion due to omissions. Therefore it is these that we must study here, for at first glance the regulations they create seem only to fill gaps, and in terms of equilibrium a gap constitutes a disturbance involving a compensating reaction only insofar as it corresponds to an already active scheme.[2]

3. Let us first recall several examples. At level I, while attempting to produce a series, the subject neglects the actual lengths of the rods, and at level II, he builds a pair, then another, by neglecting the other elements. In attempting to classify, the subject in the beginning only considers the similarities between objects. And as just mentioned, a subject watching a clay sausage being stretched out at first entirely ignores the thinning. Likewise, in the "work" experiments, the young subjects sometimes thought of the displaced objects, sometimes of the distance moved—each time omitting the other factor, the angle of impact.

How can we explain these gaps? It is clear that it is not a question of conscious choice or of intentional abstraction, since in each of these examples the regulations apparent in the following levels will reintroduce (or, more precisely, introduce) what was lacking in the initial assimilation of the facts. Although the processes in play are due in part to the conceptualizations and no longer only to the perceptions, we find ourselves confronted with a situation similar to that presented by perceptual centration, with its two fundamental characteristics: on the one hand, the impossibility, when looking or paying attention, of perceiving the whole because of the dimensions of the field; on the other, the systematic distortion due to overestimation of what is centered and devaluation of what remains in the periphery.

---

[2] For example, in the Zeigarnik effect, the gap stems from an interruption of work, and it therefore plays a role insofar as it becomes an obstacle which prevents completing the project.

Some of the first levels in the development of the ability to create series or classify are typical in this respect; unable to enlarge a field (or an "empan"[3]) at first too narrow for generalization, the subject proceeds merely by creating pairs or juxtaposing and temporarily pushes aside the other elements and their characteristics. In these centrations, which are abstract and no longer perceptual, we again find distortion caused by the overestimation of the importance of the characteristics of the objects of attention and the devaluation of the others which are not centered. In order to go beyond the mere metaphorical analogies, we must specify the dynamic quality of these processes in terms of the interactions between the adopted conceptual form and the perceived or perceptible content of the assimilated objects. In fact, the extension of conceptualization depends on its structure (as is partly the case with perception).

Consider two possibilities: either the elements (objects or characteristics) neglected are not perceived or they are perceived but pushed aside. In both cases we must explain why. If they are not perceived although perceptible, a positive factor must prevent perception. Now let us recall some of the many examples showing that the choice of what is perceived, and of what is not, is due to a guiding of perception by a superior function attributable to notions, preoperations, or operations (§17, section 3). The difference is thus less between the alternatives than we might have thought, which means that the perceptible content (perceived or not) is always present with its possible influence on the constraints exercised by the assimilating schemes. Now these constraints exist, for, unless we are totally empirical, we cannot say the scheme depends simply on a recording organ whose connections with the object are adjusted solely by the encounter (without pairing) or by a filtering without activity on the part of the subject. In fact, if the scheme retains certain characteristics of the objects, this is in virtue of the process and of an internal organization which makes

---

[3] Span of perception.——*Trans.*

them assimilable but which, by the very fact, exercises a negative pressure on the separate delements.[4] This pressure is therefore comparable to a kind of frustration and does not arise from cognitive forms of contradiction or from incompatibilities such as develop when the extension of a sausage is conceived in a manner that excludes its thinning. In this case, the centered element (extension) is valued and retained by the scheme, which confers on it a certain power supported by all the perceptible contents, while, to avoid the simple opposition becoming contradiction, the noncentered and devaluated elements are subject to a negative action which pushes them back.

4. We would expect the equilibrium thus achieved between the conceptualized form and the perceived content to be unstable for two obvious reasons. The first is that activities opposed to those of the content which modify the form are going to correspond to the constraints, whether the constraints increase value and reinforce (internally) or, on the contrary, repress and allow the form to influence the content. This content remains furnished with potentially perceivable observables (which are perhaps unconsciously perceived, as could be shown by research on their "*subception*"). The second reason for instability is that the form, that is, the scheme, remains active and can therefore be modified under the effect of new relations or coordinations which attentuate or eliminate the opposition or contradiction and make possible the liberation of new observables. It is obvious that the passage from the initial state, with some elements valued and others dismissed, to the final state, with certain of the original elements retained and some new ones probably added and conceptualized on an equal level, will be ensured by normal regulations. Since it is no longer a

4 K. H. Pribram has shown that the cortex exercises control of inputs and adjusts "previously the receptive mechanism in such a way that certain inputs become stimuli" and others are eliminated. (Proceedings of the International Congress of Psychology, held in Moscow, 1966.)

question simply of filling gaps but of lessening the repression of the elements which earlier were set aside, the disturbance can be attributed to the nascent power of these elements, which tend to penetrate into the field of recognized observables,[5] and the compensation will then consist in modifying the disturbance until it becomes acceptable. As this modification requires a construction which, however modest, means to some extent reorganizing the conceptualization, we have here another example of a construction stemming from a compensation.

§23/   The Regulations Related to the Observables on the Action (Obs. S) and the Awareness

We will now discuss the same questions but focus on the observables noted by the subject on his own actions, the

[5] As an example of this tendency of an element, at first "frustrated," to penetrate the field of perceived observables, we can refer to the following experiment. A child holds a glass, bottom up, against the ground. A marble strikes the glass, and another marble which lay up against the glass on the other side moves away. The child will say that the glass was displaced, whereas he certainly perceived it to be immobile, since he pressed it down hard. In such situations we must distinguish between the conceptualized observable although false, i.e., the glass in motion, and the observandum actually perceived, i.e., the immobile glass, with all the possible intermediaries between the "subception" and the perception, and all the possible degrees of actualization of the observable (which are not effective until about the age of ten or twelve). Moreover let us add that in our view the "subception" is probably not an "unconscious" perception, as is usually said, but a perception of which our consciousness is simply short and evanescent for lack of integration into the conceptualized consciousness. For example, I often take out my watch and look at the hands without verbal translation. Since it is not before me I take out my watch again a few minutes later and then remember having previously looked at it. My visual perception therefore was not unconscious, since there was memory with delay, but suggests a primary state of consciousness without conceptualized "awareness," and therefore without the integration which would make it knowledge (as opposed to a mere perception).

Obs. S, and no longer on the observables on the objects, *Obs. O*. We are again confronted with the fearful question of the conceptualization of the awareness (since it expresses motivation through representations[6]). The problem is again one of understanding the relations between a form and a content. Here the content is the whole set of sensorimotor processes which produce action, and the form is the system of concepts used by the subject to become aware of this action; therefore, to conceptualize this activating content. The preceding analysis may help us understand, if we have already granted a virtual content formed by the object's perceivable characteristics, a certain power of reaction to the constraints of the form. It goes without saying that this rather daring interpretation ceases to appear bold when the content no longer is what the subject perceives or can perceive of the object but is linked to what he does or knows how to do; i.e., the content is modified by motivation as such.

1. But the paradox is that the observables *Obs. S* (here they must be distinguished from the coordinations, *Coord. S*, whose activity and power are considerable) are at first considerably poorer and less complete than the observables on the object (*Obs. O*). Their initial gaps are therefore posed in more complex terms than the gaps in the observables on the object. It will be interesting to determine if these gaps are the result of regulations and compensations of the same type as cause gaps in the *Obs. O*. Let us note that during the first stages of the *Obs. S* the action is faster than the thought, so that the *Obs. S* must be incomplete. We recalled in §16 the result of the coordinations and sensorimotor regulations used during the first eighteen months of existence. Until rather late the child is capable of achieving a certain number of practical goals without knowing how they are accomplished. It is true that we often use the term "practical intelligence" in connection with the solution of

---

[6] See our work *La prise de conscience*, Presses Universitaires de France, 1974.

problems demanding concrete operations, but we do not thereby offer an explanation, and an explanation is required for an understanding of actions similar to those obtained in operational tests in general. When we succeed in separating the action itself from its verbal or graphic counterpart, we note how much the conceptualization lags behind the sensorimotor achievements. Our task, therefore, is to analyze the nature of these delays, the method of regulations leading to raising them and to the completion of the observables, *Obs. S,* and finally to establish whether or not the *Obs. S* are analogous to what we have already noted concerning observables on the object.

2. Let us first recall several examples. When we ask children to roll a Ping-Pong ball so that it will return to its point of departure, scarcely a single child succeeds. Often as early as the age of five or six a child easily manages to imitate an adult's action. However, it is only at about the age of ten or eleven that a child can adequately describe what he has done. Using a stud attached to the end of a wire (sling) a child is asked to make a circular movement with this wire, then release the wire at a good spot so that the stud reaches a box. Success is obtained by children as young as seven or eight years of age (without an example to imitate). On the other hand, the child believes that he has released the stud opposite the box, and it is only at ten or eleven that he can correctly describe the tangential movement which is essential to his success. Likewise, when we ask young children to use a pencil, to push a small plate in an oblique direction, they achieve in action all kinds of coordinations between their movements and the rotations of the plates, but without being aware of or conceptualizing these relations which they nevertheless know how to use.

A few conclusions can clearly be drawn from these facts. First, what the subject has retained of his action and conceptualized (in other words, what he has centered, valued, and not dismissed) is reduced entirely to what at first was assimilable and comprehensible. When using the Ping-Pong ball, he clearly sees that he throws it forward by pressing on the back. When using the sling, he clearly sees that he must turn the stud and release it in a manner determined by the location of the box the stud is supposed to hit.

Second, we must remember that an essential part of the action, though well executed, escapes his awareness. While using the Ping-Pong ball, the child manages to note (but not always at once) that he presses on its rear part, but he is not aware of making it rotate in a direction opposite to that in which it first moves. He believes that he merely sends it forth and that the ball, at the end of its run forward, returns by itself within a hand's distance. In the experiment with the sling, the subject thinks that he has released the mass so that it leaves its circular course at the point nearest the box. And, as mentioned earlier when the subject pushes with tools, he does not notice the various coordinations between his motions and the rotations of the object which he has put into action. Why, we may ask, are these gaps accompanied by distortions?

In these examples, it is clear that the subject does not simply neglect elements or make incomplete conceptualizations or he would have been unable to note everything at once. In these situations a greater focusing is apparent. The missing perception was actually dismissed because it was contradictory to a frequently used conceptual scheme. In fact, to make a ball turn back when it goes forward appears contradictory. The same is true of the tangential course of the stud because, for the subject, the arrival of the stud in the box implies the shortest route to the box. However, in the experiment where there seems to be a mere omission, as during the pushing with tools, the coordinations unnoticed by the subject are those which he considers nonrealizable (because he still understands only motions without rotations or the opposite), hence incompatible with the facts.

Third, it is worth stating that these elements somewhat removed from awareness are indeed the objects of a kind of repression or inhibition.[7] Of course, the subject does not begin by consciously suggesting a backward rotation for the ball or a tangential departure for the stud in order to study it reflectively and then to dismiss it as contradictory. We could then say that if he does not make such suggestions it is simply that he does not understand the possibility, and that in this case the so-called contradiction is merely due to a defect of assimilation.

Our understanding of the awareness of the action proper comes easily. We know the subject has understood something of the notion which he refuses to admit in its conceptualization, as he has used it in action, that is, in the form of a sensorimotor scheme and not of a notion. It is therefore not only legitimate but obligatory to accept that this scheme (the "know-how"), whose existence is not challenged as a scheme of action (since it has been used and consequently must have been constructed), is eliminated from conscious conceptualization by a kind of active rejection or repression because it is incompatible with other adopted concepts.

3. In short, if we distinguish the content as sensorimotor and the form as the conceptualization required by the awareness, it seems clear that we find ourselves confronted with two distinct kinds of equilibrium. In the one case, the form assimilates certain elements of the content, so that there is an equilibrium, but by mutual support or adaptive compensation;[8] each assimilating concept corresponds to an accommodation imposed by the assimilated content, and both are balanced by reciprocal adjustment. In the other case, the form rejects certain elements of the content, so that the force exerted by the form in this rejection is opposed to that which is characteristic of the content. It is

[7] See our lecture "Inconscient affectif et inconscient cognitif" given in 1970 at the Congress of the American Psychoanalytic Association and published in French, in *Raison présente*, No. 19.

[8] In Chapter one this was called "compensation by reciprocity."

interesting that in this situation of unstable equilibrium,
contrary to the preceding more stable state, the conceptualization (or form) resists, and the content exerts pressure
in opposition to this resistance. That is why we believe that
the situation is the same as that for the observables on the
object *Obs. O*. We recall that for the parts of the object
(content) conceptualized by the form, there can be equilibrium by mutual compensation between assimilation by
the form and accommodation imposed by the content.
Likewise, an unstable equilibrium can occur between the
resistance of the form (rejection of other parts of the content) and the tendency of neglected observables to conquer
the resistance. In fact, just as with the action proper, certain
schemes, used in a sensorimotor manner but not conceptualized, exert pressure on the conceptualizations and tend to
shake their repression. Therefore the object, which is manipulated in a sensorimotor manner before lending itself to
the conceptualization, includes a certain number of latent or
virtual observables due to (or made sensitive by) this
sensorimotor manipulation (therefore the likelihood of the
existence of "subceptions") which exert pressure against the
repression.

At this point we better understand the role of regulations
which, during awareness of the action proper (*Obs. S*) or
awareness of the objects (*Obs. O*), makes the observable go
from the virtual or latent state to the present or conceptualized state. The equilibrium between the conceptual form
which rejects such a latent observable (although it continues to exist at the sensorimotor level) and the pressure
exerted by this content is stable for a remarkable reason: if
we consider the conscious notions in play in the conceptualization, the potential observable tends to force the door of
consciousness, creating a disturbance, and the compensation
therefore consists first in cancelling, then in denying it by
means of the rejection (type a behavior, see §13). On the
other hand, the sensorimotor activities build up pressure on
the concepts, and it is the repression of concepts exerted by

the activities which constitutes the disturbance. The compensation will consist in the action in the opposite direction which will conquer this rejection. It is therefore clear that the ultimate regulation will mean a reinforcing of this compensation, which remains nonoperational at the first level but becomes operational under the effects of the compensating regulation. Moreover, this regulation is formative, since conquering the repression involves a modification of the opposing conceptualization and, on a restricted terrain, it imposes a reorganization, which is a construction.

4. These various remarks on awareness (*Obs. S*) lead, as we have said elsewhere,[9] to a discussion of the interpretation of some observations which Claparède has suggested. We know that based on a fine experiment on the awareness of differences between two objects (more or less easily formulated by young children) and the consciousness of similarities (far more difficult to achieve, although the subjects were old enough to tend to generalize to the utmost: to use the similarities), Claparède stated a "law" according to which awareness occurs only when there is loss of adaptability (here the differences as opposed to the generalizations), and awareness does not intervene—since it would not be needed—when the usual methods, already adapted, suffice.

Following Claparède's publication, we remarked that the loss of adaptability occurs on the periphery of the action (where contacts are made with the object), and that the zone where the functioning occurs without obstacles is that of the mechanisms internal to the action. We could therefore make a more general statement, supporting the fact that awareness proceeds from the periphery to the center—stemming from the results of the action and then moving to its internal mechanisms. But the present analysis forces us, it seems, to make some correction and at the same time furnishes us with additional enlightenment. To begin with this new insight, we can say that awareness of actions—espe-

---

[9] See our study *La prise de conscience*, the general conclusions.

cially their sensorimotor aspects—does not consist of simple
perception of all the aspects or actions, but it necessarily
implies a conceptualization. If this is so, we then understand
that the periphery of the action gives rise to easier conceptualizations than the more intimate methods of functioning. The awareness of the central aspects therefore requires
a superior reflexive work (and more complex regulations as
we will soon see).

However, regarding the periphery itself, we now know
that everything is not accessible to awareness, and that this
is particularly evident at contact points with the object
where the loss of adaptability is greatest (e.g., backward
rotation of the ball moving forward, tangential course of
the stud). Awareness is blocked because of the contradictions we have indicated. However, given a conceptualized
necessity, there is an apparent exception, for a reflexive
reorganization is indispensable in these situations (as opposed to situations with immediate conceptualizations), as
though a going back to the internal and almost operational
compositions of the action were required (which is, moreover, partly the case). On the whole, we can say that
awareness is inversely proportional to the degree of reflexive thought[10] it requires. There is little awareness during a
simple conceptualization—that is, direct application of a
form to a content (which we usually find at the periphery
of the action)—but more awareness with more difficult, and
consequently delayed, reflexive conceptualization on internal compositions (preoperational or operational, that is, on
contents which themselves are forms and are also more developed). This implies the reorganization of an initial
conceptualization (i.e., a new form dealing with a content
which is already a form).

[10] Reflexive thought being a concept of the second or nth power.

§24/   *The Regulations Dealing with the Relations between the Observables*

Having studied the regulations on the observables on the object, *Obs. O*, and on the action, *Obs. S*, it is now worth analyzing the regulations dealing with the relation between observables, and in particular between the *Obs. O* and *Obs. S*, and following their paths, *OS* or *YZ*, during types II interactions (§10 to 13). These regulations take multiple forms, but we must carefully distinguish them from regulations dealing with coordinations (*Coord. S* or *Coord. O*). The latter, by definition, include necessary inferences and therefore extend beyond the boundaries of the observable, whereas the relations between observables—even if they reach the level of quantified functions,[11] therefore lawful predictability—are themselves observables, and, if inferences are made, they must be inductive, that is, unnecessary and consist of simple generalizations of observables. The model of type II interactions distinguishes by method (although in fact this is not easy) the relations between the *Obs. O* and *Obs. S*. Resulting are the course *OS*, and the coordinations coming from the arrangements of these relations or, more precisely, inferred from them, and the courses *Obs. S* (linked to *Obs. O*) to *Coord. S* and *Coord. S* to *Coord. O*—that is, *SO* (quite distinct but inverse to *OS*). Therefore, what we are discussing here only concerns the relations between the *Obs. S* and the *Obs. O* or those between the two paths (*SO* and *OS*), but does not yet concern the coordinations in the strict sense.

  1. Before turning to the problems which are central for a theory of equilibration, the regulations inherent in the relational situations of contradictions, and the differentiation of notions initially all inclusive but virtually contradictory, we must first discuss the construction of immediately coherent

---

[11] Needless to say, we always take this term in the ordinary sense without reference to the notions of quanta or discontinuities.

relations, since they express liaisons which the subject can easily grasp. However, the problem for us is to establish whether these elementary constructions already compensate disturbances—in other words, whether the regulations present at this elaboration of constructions, by successive corrections, are already compensating.

Unfortunately it is extremely difficult to analyze the first conceptual assimilations, because the child who is just beginning to speak (which is the most interesting moment for these assimilations) is unable to explain himself or reply to questions. Consequently, much research must be carried out with children from one and a half to four years of age. But restricting ourselves to a few early notions, we can at least say that in contrast to the limited but remarkable coherent organization of sensorimotor schemes at stage VI of the preverbal period of development, the first conceptual schemes are frequently conflicting. The first form of these conflicts is seen during the use of concepts partly constructed by the subject which are then modified by the two contrary requirements of stability and plasticity. For example, one of our children designated under the term "Vouvou" first someone's dog seen from a balcony (this on several separate occasions), then figures on a carpet, next the dog owner without the dog, and finally horses, chariots, and practically any large animal or vehicle seen from the same balcony. When the conceptual significance of words is later stabilized under the constraint of social communication, the conflict reappears in a derivative form. A conceptual term can then either be used for one individual item (identical to itself) or another item representing the same category. One solution is a compromise, in which the designation remains midway between being a reference to a unique item and being a generic term by possessing flexibility and functioning as an exemplar. A child of three, for example, will ask if a new orange, separated from a preceding one by a long interval, is the same orange; yet he may consider his nanny two distinct persons according to whether she is in Geneva or in the city where his grandparents live. When questioned, children of about four hesitate between "a" and "the" moon, and often believe that shadows produced on the table come from "below the trees," and that the drafts created by moving objects are caused by the "wind" introduced into the room despite closed windows. The assimilation of shadows produced on the table and those from below the trees, as well as the identification of a draft with wind, are perfectly correct if the special cases depend on categories for a single item for lack of generic categories. Given this situation, the child makes these assimilations from a kind of interaction between the individual objects themselves.

It is therefore by no means metaphoric to speak of disturbances when a new object confronts those already assimilated to a conceptual scheme. The play of regulations then involves measuring the identities and equivalences or differences as a function of the object's resistance to the variable assimilating tendencies. To understand the development of the concept of identity, we closely studied[12] the difficulties posed for young subjects when a liquid changes form in passing from one container to another, when a piece of straight wire is bent, or when a living creature changes in size during growth. Even identity, despite the evidence acquired sooner or later in these situations, results therefore from a compensation, by no means immediate, which, for a single object, opposes modifications of form or size. Equally important, the differences can also require regulations opposing compensations which would favor the assimilation. We have seen the difficulty in classification of balancing the differences with the similarities (§20), and the difficulty in seriation, at level I, of determining differences of length when an assimilating tendency imposes the primacy of equivalences (§21). The "Vouvou" example just mentioned shows how far these equivalences can be generalized when compensations do not moderate the differences.

[12] See Volume XXIV of *Etudes d'épistémologie génétique*.

If we wish to determine in each case the reasons for successful identification of differences or equivalences, we must again refer to the equilibrium between form and content mentioned in the preceding paragraph. The same methods for increasing importance or repression enter into play when the acceptance or refusal of one special observable is in question.

2. Notable progress in the use of regulations is to be seen when the qualifications which express similarities and differences as functions (disturbances and compensations) of the conceptual assimilation are no longer derived directly from the contents but include forms derived from the preceding contents—in other words, when there is a beginning of conceptualizations of conceptualizations. This is evident when the similarities and differences are conceived as variable, when degrees intervene ("large," "quite large," "very large," etc.) which actually are differences of differences or of similarities. These are not yet comparative terms, and the relation is far from being entirely relative, but it is the beginning of this kind of organization.

Here we again find an example of the passage from absolute predicates to relational structures. But if this vocabulary is convenient in thinking of the verbal forms used, we must nevertheless specify the meanings. The qualifications constructed or used by the subject in these elementary conceptualizations of similarities and differences are both predicates, although poorly regulated for lack of hierarchies (these will be formed later, based on extensions). The qualifications are also relational, but "prerelatal" for lack of reciprocities, etc., and above all, for lack of degrees ("more or less") and a continuum for these degrees which allows seriation. They therefore remain absolute because of the gaps between them and the lack of differentiation.

Let us note, however, that once two categories are opposed by their elements' qualifications, x and y ($y = non\text{-}x$), the elements themselves can be distinguished within each category by similar contrasts. In this case, the contrast of x and *non-x* found within the x category contains a contradiction (or pseudocontradiction) which can be resolved only by giving a nuance to the qualification—that is, by introducing a qualification of the qualification for which the terms "very little x," "quite x," etc., or "very y," "quite y," etc., are used.

These degrees undoubtedly come from the regulation itself. The regulation, which consists in compensating a disturbance, first leads to this elaboration by an assimilation (permitting similarities) or a rejection followed by an assimilation to an opposite scheme (designating differences). But if these assimilations are not immediate and there is a preliminary regulation, it begins with more or less advanced compensations. Therefore, in itself, it must include degrees and oscillations between "more" and "less." The awareness of this gradation is inherent to the regulation when the content to be assimilated includes elements with intermediary qualifications—expressed by even more incomplete conceptualizations verbalized as "a little bit," "quite," "very," etc.—that can remove the contradictions.

3. We are now faced with the central problem raised by the regulation of the regulations between observables—a problem which was already broached in connection with observables conceptualized singly (§22 and 23). We are referring to the regulation of contradictions or of pseudocontradictions. First, it is clear that any regulation at any level includes a certain understanding of incompatibility. To compensate a disturbance by a modification of the meaning of the particular contrast is both to recognize an opposition, if not to constitute it, and to tend to remove it. The first result is that the relations of similarities and differences can be applied to two individual elements (or to two schemes), without which there would be contradiction. As we have seen in our experiments with seriation, it is at the elementary level that a subject does not consider that an object may be found both larger than another and smaller than a third, since it could not be simultaneously large and small. The compensation is therefore complete and even supercomplete, since it is formed merely to avoid a pseudo-

contradiction. In the case of actual contradictions, it remains incomplete (as for example in considering small boats floating because they are light and large ones not sinking although they are heavy) for lack of adequate compensation.

For the moment let us remain with pseudocontradictions. With the beginning of gradations, mentioned in section 2, the conception of contradiction develops. Let us suppose that, objectively, the possible variation for a set is distributed between one and ten. The young subject will then divide the elements of the set into a $1–5 = x$ category and a $6–10 = y$ category ($y = $ *non-x*. At first each element of one of the collections, x or y ($y = $ *non-x*), is a disturbance for the other, and each of the two schemes x and y plays a compensating role. Later, relations of differences and similarities are established within the two schemes, and quite elaborately, since each element is ever so slightly different from the others. Finally there will be as many subschemes as individual objects (labeling). In this case, since the compensating instruments, i.e., the x and the y assimilating schemes, have become supple and enriched, there will be a tendency to extend their action. And since they perform in opposite directions, this will necessitate the assimilation of reciprocals. Although the attributes x and y do not overlap, the distance between neighboring categories in x or y is less; that is, the difference, for example, between "very small" and "very, very small," begins to disappear. The boundaries between x and y will finally overlap and give rise to intersections. For example, "not very small" may get very close to "not very big" so that both might be included in a subcategory using both the "small" and "large" designations. From this we get the formation of "averages" (a term at first predicative which later acquires a semirelative meaning).

The advantage which marks this beginning of intersection is that, in its interior, and only in this restricted sector, a weak difference becomes bound up with a certain (and rather important) similarity, which is exactly the double characteristic finally attributed to the "averages." Hence we have two stages. During the first, one of the schemes, x and y, assimilates all the elements using degrees of the attribute in question. If the child begins with y (the attribute "large"), as y increases, the x (the attribute "small") becomes less and less; if the child begins with x, the opposite situation exists. The subject has to make a conceptualization of a conceptualization (modify x or y with "more" or "less") and generalize it for the whole set, but at first he does not know how to turn to two kinds of comparisons at once. During the second stage he will succeed. Each relation of "less than" he will be able to equate with a "greater than" in such a way that $2 < 3$ (using x, "smallness") is equivalent to $8 > 7$ (using y, "largeness") (in the seriation of ten elements starting from both ends of the course). Here, in fact, is the level of the operational seriation with its rational characteristic, its reversibility, and its transitivity—the final products of previous regulations (§21).

The point of departure of this evolution is the regulations which, for a given content, oppose relations of similarity (hence impose an assimilating form) in compensation of disturbances produced by the elements or aspects of this content which resist and impose relations of difference (hence oppose the assimilation to a scheme x for the transfer on y (*non-x*), when the content would be distorted (for lack of accommodation) if it were assimilated in x. This being so, the construction starts with the two schemes x and *non-x* (y) which are noncontradictory when they apply to different objects but which appear contradictory (pseudo-contradiction) when they concern the same object. The evolution of this initial regulating process leads from these two disjointed collections (under x and y) to increasing intersections, and finally to identification by reciprocal assimilation of the two categories, and to a comprehension—since a small difference is equivalent to a large similarity and reciprocally—with complete compensation of the relations "less than" and "greater than."

Let us now consider actual contradictions, as in the ex-

ample of the small and large boats, in which the two initial
categories, x and y (light and heavy), include more than
two attributes, and the concepts used are heterogeneous because they are undifferentiated. The light boat is not strong
but is carried by the water which is strong, whereas the
heavy boat is strong and can ride the water alone. The
notion of heaviness thus implies the concept of strong, and
heaviness includes multiple components (whether it is the
water which "carries" the boat or the boat which "carries"
itself). It is remarkable that, despite this essential difference,
the regulations which gradually lead the child to overcome
these contradictions are similar to those that enable him to
free himself of pseudocontradictions. In applying the same
method of progressive compensations between the more and
the less, the subject cannot help understanding, since the
method leads in certain cases to acceptable consequences
(coherent relations), whereas in others the compensations
or symmetries remain incomplete and the consequences
absurd.

To return to our example, if the heaviest is quite the
equivalent of the lightest, the quality of "better holding on
the water" is not "to be less borne by the water," since
there are two factors, the water and the boat, and the notion of force is taken in two distinct meanings, to carry and
to be carried. If the subject proceeded by degrees as in a
seriation, he would arrive at the conclusion that halfway to
the extreme conditions the median boat would no longer
toss on the water, since it is too heavy and would not hold
itself sufficiently because it is too light. Consequently, when
he wishes to generalize the relation between the force of the
water and the weights of the boats, the child will say that
the water always carries the boats. He will then say, if it
carries the large ones, it is because they are "light for the
lake" although "heavy" for us. Finally the subject suggests
the notion of weight relative to volume and thus reaches entire compensations: less heavy $\times$ larger = heavier $\times$ smaller.

In this case, the two initial categories of heavy and light
finally merge into an overall category of weights relative to

volumes, with reciprocity of the relations "greater than" and "less than," but the concepts of size, weight, and force will give rise to differentiated subcategories, with distinct but coherent relations, as dictated by their various meanings. The elimination of actual contradictions seems to be dependent on the same compensations between relations as the pseudocontradictions, and to require the same successive modes characteristic of the initial regulations and of the final operational symmetries.

4. We are thus led to the question of the functional relationships or dependencies between variables whose roles are evident in the preceding example. First let us return to the levels studied under sections 2 and 3 where the initial overall relations begin to be quantified in terms of more or less. The moment a difference is recognized as variable, thereby incorporating a quantity, the subject becomes capable of noticing the possible link between two distinct series of variations, which constitutes a function. The link can be between an event B and its cause A, in which case the suppression of A involves suppression of B (*sublata causa, tollit effectus*[13]). In addition, variations of A and B may be noted to have other effects so that each value of A may correspond to one of C. Between the ages of five and a half and seven these covariations then involve the formation of simply qualitative functions and ordinal correspondences, without conservation, which will be modified to form quantitative functions at the outset of the level of operational compositions and conservations.

In a study of regulations, the functions are of special interest. The subject discovers them only by groping either through varying the observables on the object, thus altering the relations between objects (model IIC, §12, function xy), or through an adjustment of the action proper as in the model IIB and above all in IIA (§11 and 10), where the results, *Obs. O*, are functions of adjustments of the actions as recognized by the *Obs. S*. If the relations between objects are

---

[13] Once the cause is removed, the effect disappears.——*Trans.*

varied, the variations of the independent variable x, in $y = f(x)$, can be called disturbances insofar as they modify the previous state, and the variations of y (dependent variables) will be the compensations which conserve the relation. Obviously, if during the function-discovery phase the subject proceeds from variations of y to those of x, from the viewpoint of his awareness the roles are reversed.

But the relations between the *Obs. O* and the *Obs. S* are far more complex when the action proper intervenes as a factor. As we stated in §23, awareness generally proceeds from the periphery results of the action in the direction of its (central) mechanism. The results themselves are often difficult to analyze. Consequently, while aiming for a result, conceived overall as a function of his action, the subject can at first be rather ignorant of the mechanisms at work.

The subject then can undergo one of two experiences. First, the action can be seen as a failure and thereby necessitate a better active adjustment; that is, the object's variations appear as disturbances, and the corrections due to the adjustment of the action are compensating. But since only the observables on the object can make it possible to rectify the observables on the action, the *Obs. S* depend on the *Obs. O* and again compensate their variations (which are disturbing as compared to the previous *Obs. O* and *Obs. S*). For example, a subject begins by being unsuccessful when he tries to reach a target with a ball after it has ricocheted off a wall. In this example, the point on the wall hit by the ball plays a disturbing role and the subject will adjust his aim accordingly (compensation); but not knowing if he should adjust his aim to the left or right of the preceding point, he uses verifications on the object (*Obs. O*) to correct the observables on the action (*Obs. S*).

Or subject can find the action succeeds more easily and there is no greater awareness, hence adequate conceptualization of its functioning. Once again it is the observables on the object (*Obs. O*)—which by conceptual regulation this time and no longer by conscious physical adjustment as in the preceding case—which make it possible to correct the errors on the *Obs. S* by a play of compensations. For example, in the preceding situation involving ricochets, it is the variations in the tests, even when successful, which enable the subject to be aware of the changes in the orientation of his movements (as a function of the angles of incidence and reflection). We then see why, in model IIA (§10), we consider the direction *OS* in the relations between the two kinds of observables, *Obs. O* and *Obs. S*, as usually primary to the direction *SO*.

In conclusion, the study of regulations of relations between the observables shows that, no less than during conceptualization of initial observables (§22 and 23), the constructions required for the passage from one level of development to another are orientated by the compensations.

§25/   *The Regulations of Coordinations* (Coord. S *and* Coord. O)—I: *The Causality*

But what about the coordinations themselves, that is, the inferential mechanisms that are parts of the whole cognitive structure? Will the equilibration by progressive regulations here be found to be merely a secondary and corrective mechanism, intervening after each attempt at construction, to improve the form and the functioning, or will it appear again as formative and constructive insofar as any cognitive construction requires a compensating dimension which is complementary (in the double psychogenetic and logical sense) to the characteristics of the constructive novelty? We will try to show that if compensating mechanisms still exist in the complete cognitive structures, this is because the logical and validly deductive functioning which they ensure in these states of final closing is the result of the continuous progress in the compensations revealed by the regulations in play during the formation periods. The compensation, so to speak, is both cause and effect or, if we prefer, factor for and result of structurations; cause or factor during forma-

tive regulations and effect or result when an integral part of
the final structure.

1. The situation is clearest in the field of causal explanation. On the one hand, causality consists essentially of a
system of compensations between what the active factor
loses and what the passive factor(s) gains. On the other
hand, the conceptualization of causality arises within the
subject's movements and the modifications noted on the object. The final structures are therefore prepared at the outset, since the regulations apply to the physical movements
even before they are internalized. However, in logico-
mathematical structures, the final operational compensations
result from those that make up the internal mechanism of
any regulation and not from the physical effects (as related
to the acts of conceptualizations) as is the case with causality.

Causality begins at the start of the sensorimotor and perceptive levels, and from the moment of formation of the
elementary schemes, especially the tactile-kinesthetic, it is
possible to distinguish: (1) the regulations dealing with the
observables as such—these are not yet conceptualized (since
there are no concepts at this stage), but directly perceived
and schematized during their repetitions; and (2) the regulations dealing with the coordinations as compositions
which go beyond the boundaries of the observables. If we
refer to the model of interaction IA (§9), we distinguish as
observables on the action (*Obs. S*) the movements, Ms, and
the thrusts, Ps, made by the subject, and on the object
(*Obs. O*) the resistance, Ro, and the movements, Mo, of the
object acted upon. This being so, we have seen that the
regulations on the observables of the action consist: (*a*) in
an adjustment of effort, that is, in a measure of the movements, Ms, and thrusts, Ps, but as a function of the resistance, Ro, of the object (arrow *a* on the diagram in §9);
and (*b*) in relating the object's movements, Mo, and those
of the subject, Ms, the relation can be seen to be functional,
as the more the Mo increase, the more the Ms increase
(arrow *b* on the diagram). It is therefore clear that these

regulations on the observables are compensating, which is well known in regard to the use of effort and is evident also for the movements.

The coordinations which result (interaction IIA of §10) constitute the causal link, for if we turn to the preceding observables, and even to their regulations, we find merely regular successions with no causal necessity whatever. The more the object resists, the more the subject pushes, and the more the subject advances, the more the object is displaced. As Hume has shown,[14] these are only "conjunctions" with no "connection" at all. It is then that the coordinations intervene, due to the inferences of the subject (*Coord. S*) which, however, are attributed to the object (*Coord. O*). The subject comes to the conclusion, but without perceiving directly or acknowledging a visible or invisible transfer, that since the two functions *a* and *b* (arrows *a* and *b* in the model discussed in §9) something has been "transmitted from him to the object or in a general way from the agent to the passive object.

In this event, how do we describe this transmission which is both production (insofar as the subject is modified) and conservation (insofar as the transmitted movement is inherited from the productive movement)? We again have to admit, because of the inferential composition and no longer for a verification, a play of compensations: what has been gained by the subject (the movements *Mo*) is lost or spent by the agent, and it is this necessary compensation which, at every level interpreted, is found again in various conceptualizations up to the conservation of the quantity of the transmitted movement, *mv*, and of the transferred kinetic energy ($\frac{1}{2}mv^2$). At the sensorimotor and perceptive levels an inferential or preinferential composition already exists, and the regulations inherent in the sensorimotor simplification or in the perception which ensure it are already com-

---

[14] Moreover, if we equate the subject with a billiard ball the four observables remain the same except that simple functional variations are substituted for active regulations.

pensating. For sensorimotor schemes of causality, this is easy to prove by following the progress of the increasing "spatialization" and objectification of causality (§16) with their effect on the tactile-kinesthetic-perceptual causality. With the visual perception of causality, it is equally clear that the "impression" of causality is a result and does not correspond to the perception of a transfer process (*phi* movement, etc.) actually seen to occur between the agent and the subject. This impression is therefore the product of the regulations of perception dealing with the direction and speed of ocular movements. For example, when the eye follows the agent's movement and then goes to the object, there is an "ocular transport," both of the direction of movement and the speed, accomplished in such a manner that if the passive element is slower than the active there is simultaneous perception of a resistance[15] and a continuity. Thus it is these regulations of perceptions which ensure the compositions, with, notably, the "preinferences" they involve (in the Helmholtz sense, which is accepted today), in such a manner that, even on this elementary terrain, causality must be conceived as a coordination (*Coord. S*), and not as an observable, if we distinguish the directly perceived observables as individual and localized, and their effect as overall.

2. In the superior or notional forms of causality, we again find the subject's inferential coordinations (*Coord. S*), but their results are attributed to the object itself (*Coord. O*). We can also see the structure of their compensations which are prepared or ensured by the already compensating regulations. For example, in the understanding of the successive coordinations leading to the mediate transmission of motion, the subject who succeeds in conceiving of the motion as an external connection of immediate transmissions (once he has realized that all the marbles do not move and that the

---

[15] Resistance perceived, through a proprioceptive mechanism, from the slowed-down ocular movement and through a visual mechanism responding to the moving object itself.

one he shoots does not follow the others) cannot make the proposition of successive shocks, initiated with the moving marble and transmitted from marble to marble, without compensating the departure movement of the last passive marble with what the preceding ones have done. When the comprehension of the semi-internal mediate transmission begins, inspired by the operational transitivity, this correction of the preceding conceptual scheme satisfies the subject, because a transmission passing "through" the objects suggests by its very nature something that every active marble "gives" ("it has given its élan"), and which can be gained by the one that takes it.

To express these levels in terms of type α and type γ behaviors (§13), let us note that the disturbing factor, as compared to the precociously acquired scheme of immediate transmission arises from the presence of the intermediary elements between the end marbles, which we will call A and N. On the initial level they are neglected (type α behavior), which means that the disturbance is avoided. Later there is both integration of the disturbance (type β behavior), since the intermediaries give rise to a conception of linkage and immediate transmissions, and distortion of observables, since the marbles are "seen" to move. This imagined movement is interesting from the viewpoint of the functional compensations, mentioned in §13, because if the initial movement is supposed to increase, the same is true of its effect, whereas if it is assumed done away with, the transmission is also (*sublata causa*). On the following level another compensable relation is added. We note that if A pushes B and if B pushes C, etc., the subject's thinking goes from C, etc., to A until he conceives of the transitivity of the shock of A on B, etc. But this transitivity remains imperfect, since the impulsion can increase or decrease during successive shocks. After a glimpse of the meaning of "reaction" (in the physical sense as compared to an act), the last level reaches the rank of type γ behaviors.

In the formation of causal explanation by accumulation of elements (corpuscular schemes), the play of compensations is equally evident. We have shown subjects sugar which melts in a glass of water by breaking down into smaller and smaller pieces. In attempting to find an explanation, the final disappearance of the pieces (which is the equivalent of a loss) is at first compensated only by overall processes such as are indicated by "They have become water" (which is a gain for the liquid), or "They disappeared into the air," even after a level of development where compensation of type a (§13) leads to a cancellation of the sugar by annihilation. But at the outset of the operational level, the compensation becomes effective with transformation of visible grains into invisible "very small grains," and conservation is bolstered by the taste of the sweetened water. In a Franklin distiller, a liquid contained at a far end of the device disappears and then reappears at the other end. Young subjects studying the apparatus, who as yet make no assumptions concerning evaporation or condensation, nevertheless imagine compensations; they speak of water which disappears from one side as having passed through the glass and dissipating into the air, and the water which can be seen at the other end (where the completely sealed tube is plunged into cold water to lower the temperature) as having entered through the glass from an outside container. At a later level, there will be exact compensation (with the conservation of matter) between the quantity of the initial liquid and that which reappears at the other end; the suggestion made that it was not noticed between one end and the other as it slipped by in the form of very fine drops, or finally in the form of vapor. But at each of these levels there is some compensation between the gains and losses.

If we use action and reaction terms, this constitutive aspect of causality is of course equally evident but acquires an exact form only on the superior levels. However, very precociously, the inferential coordinations explain the slowing down of the agent by the resistance or braking action of the passive object, which is not a compensation from the viewpoint of directions but is one for that of the conflicting forces.

In short, causality includes compensations at every level, from the outset of the elementary regulations up to the superior deductive models, and in all cases the regulations, like the deductions, deal with the object's material transformations yet themselves are the result of the subject's activities.

§*26*/   *The Regulations of Coordinations*—II: *The Logico-Mathematical Coordinations and the Form of the Regulations*

The subject's coordinations resulting in the logico-mathematical operations, the final operational structures, achieve a compensation in a complete form, as indicated by the fact that they are reversible, and compensation exists between all operations that show relations of inversion, reciprocity, or correlativity (duality). We have long presented this reversibility as a product of the equilibration which we have followed step by step during the formative stages; we have conceived the operation as a regulation which has become "perfect" insofar as it anticipates all the transformations and prevents errors. Now we must justify these propositions by describing the mechanism which connects the regulation with the operation, and show why the logico-mathematical structures result in complete compensations with generalized symmetries. Whereas causality, although it involves its special mode of compensation as a result of its structures and combined conservations, is irreversible in its time-space sequences, it consequently is only expressed in partial equivalences with the operational compositions from which it proceeds in the different forms that it attributes to objects and reality.

1. The great difference between logico-mathematical structures and causality lies in the fact that the regulations involved in the development of causality, from the beginning of the action plan proper to their use at superior levels, act on outside contents and modify them materially. On the

other hand, the regulations required for a logico-mathematical structure intervene only with their own form and draw from this form only the elements and connections which finally acquire operational characteristics, because from the outset these regulations exhibit an inherent logico-mathematical characteristic.

a. We have seen that the regulations related to the observables in a causal system act directly on their material transformations, whereas conceptualization is achieved by awareness or verifications involving measurement of the effort spent in the action proper, evaluation of the thrusts between objects, analysis of time-space sequences, speeds, etc. The regulation of coordinations (*Coord. O*) requires, for example, controlling the existence of a transmission by referring to preceding observables which are related to the object; or inferring the relations between an action and a reaction, but the input is always from observable material contents. Certainly, these deductions and inferences depend on logico-mathematical coordinations, and we will return to them. However, insofar as the links they establish are attributed to objects, that is, insofar as they are causal, they tend to join the material transformations of the objects and consequently are based on the physical contents, first observable then imagined, in the heart of or between the observables. That is why they finally lead to compensations of a material or dynamic nature.

b. On the other hand, the regulations intervening in the logico-mathematical coordinations (*Coord. S*) lead to compensations related to forms only (reversibility, reciprocity, etc.) and remain homogeneous with those in play in the regulating functioning itself, since a characteristic of any regulation is to have at the outset forms analogous to the elementary compensations. Certainly the compensations are incomplete, yet they are of almost reversible forms. This is clear regarding the regulations dealing with the preoperational or operational observables; for example, these regulations will reinforce or check a cognitive act, whether it involves arrangement, the assimilation of an observable to a conceptual scheme, or any composition at the research and groping stage. Either the regulation will imprint a certain direction on the research, or on the act being carried out which may be more or less different from the direction seen when the scheme is stabilized, or it will oscillate between one order of succession and another. Regulations concerning the coordinations themselves, during the course of their elaboration, will, *a fortiori*, in turn be reinforced or checked, directed one way or another, organized according to a given order of its opposite, etc., in order to avoid the contradictions between coordinations which at first were permitted to be heterogeneous. Such functioning arises from the very forms of any regulation, since by definition it is able to act on any content according to the symmetries related to activities already quantified in an elementary manner. These symmetries call upon reinforcement or weakening, increase or decrease, one direction or another, etc., in short, modifications in "more or less" which result in compensations.

At the outset of the sensorimotor regulations, the restricted improvements are easy to note from the retroactions and anticipations, and we find then a gradual reduction in the amplitude of their oscillations. At this time, as well as later, we observe the characteristic inherent in the regulation of being able to correct content thanks to the forms which by an adjustment of "more or less" affects compensations. Let us turn to another area: when a subject is attempting to organize a series, using only an empirical method, and finally achieves a complete ordering, the regulations not only correct each error but oscillate between the relations "greater than" and "less than," and produce a "for" or "against" at each attempted estimation so that decisions take place. Here again, if the corrections were not made according to forms which compensate themselves, these corrections would cease to be directed.

c. But, if all regulation consists in an activity of forms which compensate by the play of "more or less," the reason is, on the one hand, that the regulations, even without being operational, are of a logico-mathematical nature, and, on the other, that the regulations show the same characteristic in every field, including that of causality—or particularly in the area of causality—as the causal coordinations (*Coord. O*) are themselves inferential. Indeed these are the same regulations, with the same forms, which we find in every area of knowledge, although the difference remains essential between the situation in which they apply to a physical system and the situation in which they apply to a logico-mathematical system. In the second case, the regulation modifies content consisting of forms, and therefore there is homogeneity between this content (or field of application) of the regulation and the structure of the regulation. In processing direct input from the physical world, the regulation applies, as already stated, to a material content which in a sense remains outside the regulating structure. This is, of course, obvious, since the logico-mathematical structures are the result of the subject's activities and the material content is obtained from the object or from physical (and in this sense objective) characteristics of the action proper.[16] Consequently the regulation in a causal system materially modifies the content (elements of the observables can become more or less important and the objective facts can be more or less accepted or rejected as a result of coordinations), whereas in a logico-mathematical system the regulation merely modifies the forms by using its own forms.

However, since the methods of regulation remain the same in every field and are of a logico-mathematical nature, based on "more or less," symmetries, etc., the beginning of any process that yields knowledge of the physical world must include a logico-mathematical contribution and a con-

---

[16] We can associate the causal regulations of the action with Janet's affective regulations which deal with behavior's energetic quality: regulations establishing action ("erection of the tendency") or termination of action, sustaining activity (interest, ardor, effort), or checking (fatigue, etc.). It should be noted that these modifications are in + and −, and that the beginnings and the completions include also a form of cancellation, but as special cases of these + and −.

tribution which the regulation itself, if we can speak thus, attributes to its object although the object is of a material nature and outside the regulation. In other words, the moment the subject increases or decreases an aspect of a regulation (in its physical action or between objects), a logico-mathematical characteristic has been applied, but it is at once attributed to the material itself. As a result, knowledge of the physical world on every level is inseparable from logico-mathematical structures, but logico-mathematical knowledge can be separated from the comprehension of the physical world, and sooner or later leads to the state of "pure" logic or mathematics.

2. We might fear that by giving regulations forms, we would be led to postulating an autonomous intelligence capability, although intelligence itself long ago ceased to be a "faculty." Can we not say that regulation can be reduced to the whole set of reactions of various elements in their setting to one another, and that these various actions then compensate themselves using their similar characteristics? This presents two kinds of difficulties. The first is that there is no compensation without compensating activity, whose initial forms are evident at the outset of the assimilation and accommodation, and at the start of the arrangement of relations between the elements. We have seen in fact that between the contents and the forms a complete equilibration (§22 and 23) intervenes which includes compensation activities. The second difficulty is that these actions and reactions of the elements of the content do not occur by chance but are influenced by the historical development, as the preceding activities influence the following ones through the progressive extension of the characteristics of retroaction and anticipation attributable to the regulation. Without taking these influences into account, we would not understand the essential fact that the oscillations characteristic of the beginnings of certain regulations are of decreasing size, and that they stabilize themselves not because of increasing disorder (entropy) but because an organization can be developed. Actually, if we were dealing with chance,

either the groping would never end or would finish in compromises, whereas it is increasingly directed. In other words, each whole set of regulations is merely a system of compensations which occur in a given context, just as each operational structure is nothing more than a system of compensable transformations occurring in a given context, but the first of these systems is already organized or being organized, even when the second is only partly so. Thus it is no metaphor to speak of regulations as systems, and to grant them more or less general forms of compensations whose activity and application prepare for the operational mechanisms which function at various levels. This hypothesis is strengthened, as we have seen in Chapter Two, by our understanding of the endogenous improvement of regulations through the process of increasing equilibrations. We will return to this later.

Let us now repeat that the regulations are the source of operations which can be called "perfect" regulations in the Ashby sense. But, what we understand more easily, if we accept the distinction between the internal form characteristic of any regulating process and the results which modify the content to which it applies, is that the operation is not derived from effective compensations to which the regulations lead in every case, but rather from internal processes used by the regulation to reach a result, since these processes initially possess logico-mathematical forms. Hence the gradations, the "more or less," which intervene in the compensations, exist at the genesis of the additive operations; the order followed in the processes will play a role in the operations of order, the symmetries in the operations of correspondence, etc.

3. It now becomes acceptable to maintain that the coordinations of the subject's actions (*Coord. S*) or, in general, the operational or logico-mathematical compositions themselves constitute constructions coming from compensations or from a search for compensations. First, each composition includes a fundamental aspect of compensation, since any necessary inference and any logic are based on

structures founded on symmetries (inverse operations, etc.).

Second—and we will restrict ourselves to commonsense remarks—it is obvious that a subject would not give himself to deductive constructions unless they answered his need. But without limiting ourselves, in the functionalist tradition, to saying that a need is the mark of a nonbalance, and that its satisfaction expresses a reequilibration, we have seen (§22 and 23) in dealing with the regulations of observables both on the object *(Obs. O)*, and again, even more clearly, on the action *(Obs. S)*, that the gaps correspond, in a cognitive field, to a complex play of notional valuing and devaluing with the dynamic quality they imply in regard to the repression of separate elements and to the pressure they can exercise on the conceptualization being organized.

We can say as much, and even more, of the regulations dealing with the coordinations. Certainly a subject is never troubled by what he completely ignores, and it is not the need of a general compensation for the huge sphere of the unknown that drives us to undertake intellectual constructions. In the zone of the infinite boundary between what is assimilated and what remains without interest, at least for the present, intervene quantities of approximate knowledge and of poorly solved problems which constantly inspire research. It is therefore in this region that the unstable play of dynamic processes develops and makes valuable certain questions while brushing aside others though not cancelling them. In fact, we never abolish a question; even thrust back, it arises by itself because of its implications which bind it to what appears resolved. It is therefore by no means tautological to imply that each new construction, including inferential coordinations, which arise from some area of study (which, for an active mind, occurs every day), aims to compensate not deficits or random gaps but those which are part of already activated schemes, hence are disturbances which until now prevented the solution of particular problems. When, for example, children, aged seven or eight, make the discovery, which is very important to them, that in any seriation or classification, the relations of the form "less than" necessarily correspond to the relations of the form "greater than," there is certainly a major compensation that follows the many disturbances involved in the simple empirical construction of series or the lack of comprehension of the quantitative relations defining inclusion (i.e., $B > A$, if $A + A = B$ and A and A' are positive quantities.)

We can now state the third argument. The justification of the link between the logico-mathematical constructions and the compensations is furnished by the analysis of regulations, since they intervene in the formative phases of any construction. As we have just seen, the internal structure of any regulation itself consists of forms which from the beginning include logico-mathematical structures of "more and less," of symmetries, etc., hence of multiple compensations between inverse or opposed elements. Given these facts, the association that we assume to exist between the regulations and the operations confirms not only the compensating characteristic of the operational structures, but also the formative and constructive role of these compensations during the entire long course leading from the elementary regulations to the superior operations.

In short, we can therefore maintain that the equilibration does not constitute a characteristic superadded to the construction of cognitive structures in general, but from the beginning of the conceptualizations of observables to the compositions of deductive forms, this equilibration is inseparable from the construction. From the psychogenetic viewpoint, the equilibration involves the driving force, since it constantly produces new formations and at the same time explains the spontaneous, and finally necessary, accession of the superior operational structures. And, from the logical viewpoint, the equilibration expresses itself in the reversibility and the constructive symmetries of these required structures.

§27/ *Conclusion*

We must now state the essence of our interpretations. The main idea is commonplace: however varied the goals pursued by action and thought (to modify inanimate objects, living objects, oneself, or simply to understand them), the subject seeks to avoid incoherence and always tends therefore to certain forms of equilibrium, at times reaching them, but using them only as temporary stages. Even logico-mathematical structures, whose closure ensures local stability, are completed only to reopen new problems as operations are performed on preceding structures. Thus the most developed science remains a continual becoming, and in every field nonbalance plays a functional role of prime importance, since it necessitates reequilibrations.

The central concept in our explanation of cognitive development (whether we speak of the history of science or of psychogenesis) is therefore that of successive improvements of the forms of equilibrium; in other words, of an "increasing equilibration." Our effort consists in seeking the mechanisms, the problem being to take into account the two inseparable aspects: the compensation of disturbances responsible for nonbalances motivating research, and the construction of novelties characterizing the increase.

The subject is subdivided as follows. Any reequilibration includes actions with their general teleologic characteristic, and we must explain the choice of goals, the newer ones being more durable, and the improvement of means or the efficiency of those already in use. The uses of three important forms of equilibrium furnish the beginning of an explanation. We merely have to consider separately (although actually they are scarcely separable) the equilibrium of relations between the subject and the objects essential for physical or experimental knowledge; the equilibrium of coordinations between schemes or between subschemes of schemes, which dominates logico-mathematical knowledge; and the general equilibrium between the whole and the parts, hence, between the differentiations of schemes or of subschemes and their integration into a total system. It is this third equilibration which, dominating the two others, although less perfect or precisely because it is more likely to be incomplete, appears to determine action finality. In fact, it is always on the occasion of a gap and as a function of disturbances that we have new research whose finality depends on the entire system in its concurrent state of inadequacy. The gap tends to be removed by differentiation, and the subject's relations with the objects and the coordinations between schemes and subschemes of the same rank furnish the means with their special goals subordinated to the general equilibration.

The crucial problem therefore is to understand the method for the improvement of regulations, in other words, the "why" of the increasing equilibrations as revealed by their construction and increased coherence. The "how" of the improvement is clear: their construction consists in the elaboration of operations dealing with the preceding constructions; there are relations of relations, regulations of regulations, etc. In short, new forms deal with previous ones and include them as contents. This elaboration remains essentially endogenous, even if an equilibrium between the subject and the objects remains constantly necessary, for the contribution from objects requires either an input from forms, from operations applied to them, or from systems of coordinations or operational compositions attributed to them. In addition, the process of this endogenous construction uses reflecting abstractions which take the elements of new forms from the heart of the most elementary ones.

The improvement of the equilibration then is possible because the superior system is the seat of new regulations and its construction includes a more complex set of assimilations and accommodations; and any scheme or subscheme at any level showing this bipolarity forms regulations (Chapter One, §6). The later schemes are richer than the preceding, since the reflecting abstraction leads to a great number of compositions and this increased wealth of regulations offers improved control. The result is a hierarchy of regulations of regulations leading (by extension of the initial cycles and multiplication of the different coordinations which require an integration of superior rank) to self-regulation and self-organization.

However, we are still faced with the "why" of these new constructions, for if the character of the operations on the operations, or of the development of forms of forms explains the improvements adequately, the reasons for their elaboration are still not explicit, and to associate them with a continual or periodic need for differentiations and integrations only displaces the problem to the causes of this need and begs the question as to why the two tendencies require balancing. The whole set of facts reviewed in Chapters Three and Four suggests an answer, since we believe that we have verified the constant unity of constructions and compensations. An equilibrium, let us recall, consists of a compensation of all the "virtual work" which is compatible with the links of the system and which is, from the cognitive viewpoint, compatible with all the modifications possible under the constituent laws of the structure. We will therefore say that in a logico-mathematical system which has achieved its closure, all *these* modifications are within it and integrated, whereas modifications that are foreign to its laws remain outside. This we understand for a given state of this system, but if we distinguish laws and their modifiable characteristics, unknown until now, or unfamiliar constituent laws of its generalized structure (the facts which it produces by its very constitution), we need to know if a system loses its essential characteristics because of being enlarged. For example, since algebra was first conceived as commutative, should we cease to speak of an algebra in case of noncommutativity? New possibilities are revealed by the constitution of a structure, which shows virtual disturbances as compared to its real state, but which can be compensated by coherent incorporations (type α and type γ behaviors, see §13). Our proposition is therefore that operations dealing *with* preceding operations owe their creation to these situations, and that the extension of the previous system consists of an improved equilibration insofar as the disturbance arising from a virtual modification is surmounted by such an incorporation. Moreover, this kind of process acquires a significance which is genetic; that is, it will be accessible at every level, even the elementary, since the virtual modification is closer to known compositions and will therefore be more easily suggested by them.

There are any number of examples. Consider the French, A_1, plus the foreigners to France, A'_1, + the Swiss, A_2, + the foreigners to Switzerland, $A'_2 + \ldots = $ all men, B. This scheme, if limited to equivalences, naturally suggests the possibility of making a list of all the possible categories and subcategories; hence, finally a classification of all the classifications or "group of parts," leading to the combination of the following stage. Likewise a seriation, in its general form, is a connection according to any order; e.g., $ABCDEF$ or $FEDCBA$. But if we can follow two orders, why not combine them in $FAEBDC$? And why not continue? In this case, we finally reach a seriation of all the seriations, hence "permutations" of the following stage. Likewise the composition of the inversions and reciprocities lead to the group $INRC$, etc. We rediscover such facts at every level, and we have seen that the principal factor in the development of sensorimotor schemes into representative concepts was the possibility of adding an assimilation of objects between them to that of the objects related solely to schemes of action. Such an addition certainly depends on this intervention of transformations, virtual until now, in the processes of the sensorimotor systems, and it should lead to a level on which multiplication of coordinations has already been achieved.

This interpretation can raise two kinds of objections. The first is that, if in this book we have taken the terms "disturbance" and "compensation" in their various meanings and related them to the very general concept of assimilation schemes (the disturbance being what creates the obstacle to reaching a goal—the compensation being what reduces this obstacle and favors reaching the goal), we have never mentioned disturbances except in regard to a real object or event. In the present context, on the contrary, the disturbance is only related to "virtual work," and itself is also virtual! If the founders of the rational method had had the courage to refer to virtual work in a discussion of the equilibrium of inert bodies, and if d'Alembert had made it one of the pivots of his system, there would be an additional reason why we conscious beings should consider the nonbalance that we experience when we have the feeling something remains to be done a fruitful state, i.e., a state in which we haven't exhausted the possible ways of reaching a goal opened by a structure completed elsewhere. The obstacle is certainly first felt only as a gap, but it becomes concrete the moment work begins and then, before it is incorporated in a superior whole, it seems to threaten the preceding completion. The special characteristic of these virtual disturbances is the result of the novelty of what is to be constructed as compared to constructions by simple adjustment, and it therefore seems legitimate for us to risk generalizations.

The other possible objection comes from the opposite direction. If the novelty to be constructed is suggested by the preceding completions, is it not predetermined? The reply is that the world of possibilities is never complete nor, consequently, given in advance (the whole of all the possibilities doubtless is a paradoxical notion, since the "whole" itself is only possible). In other words, each completion opens new possibilities which did not exist as such at the previous levels.

A next step follows easily in this explanation. If a new possibility, opened by the lower system, imposes itself at a given moment as the necessity to go beyond compensating a virtual nonbalance, it was neither formed nor did it arise by chance from the subject's spontaneous inventions, but it is a product of the multiplication of the independent subsystems which compose the whole system of real knowledge. In fact, insofar as these subsystems increase, remain distinct and specific, and develop at different speeds (characteristics which are to be expected considering the diversity of the sources of acquisition), the various nonbalances existing among them require many trials for assimilation and for reciprocal accommodation; hence, we see new possibilities of setting up a relation which will hasten the formation of these forms of forms or operations on operations that we have just discussed.[17] This is a process governed by probability and is comparable to the one described in Chapter One which controls the action of the multiplication of schemes on the increase of "accommodation standards" (§6).

Moreover, if the development of cognitive structures is due to the reflecting abstraction and to the appropriate operations, these constructive processes remain linked with the constant requirements for compensations seen in the equilibration of relations between subsystems of the same rank. But these relations depend on many equilibrations of relations between the subject and the objects, and the increasing coherence of the subsystems conditions the third kind of equilibrium which imposes itself between the general integration and the differentiations. The secret of cognitive development seems, therefore, to be found in the interconnections between these three forms of equilibrium.

But if there are three distinct varieties as defined by the content of the relations equilibrated, these three types of equilibration use a common structural mechanism. All three require increasingly complete and detailed compensations between the positive characteristics or affirmations, related both to outside facts and to conceptualizations and operations required for assimilation, and the corresponding negations also related to the objects and to the operational processes. Now, as we have seen throughout, these compen-

---

[17] One of the remarkable results of the recent research carried out by Inhelder, Sinclair, and Bovet on learning is the discovery, in situations where we expected relatively simple associations, of the existence of very numerous networks between subsystems and in forms we scarcely suspected.

sations play a determining role in any equilibration, since, at the initial stages, the affirmations and positive characteristics are of primary importance and the lack of inverse operations and adjustment, furnished by the negations or the exclusions, causes a nonbalance. These observations, analyzed in our earlier research on contradictions, are again found essential to the equilibration mechanism; on the occasion of each compensation, the equilibration requires the construction of the negation devices lacking at the beginning, whether they involve opposing categories, variations in more or less, or inverse operations in general. We have maintained at all times that the equilibration was bound up with a progressive reversibility. However, it was only in studying in detail the more advanced nature and difficulties of the elaboration of negations that this proposition could acquire concrete and verifiable significance in the analysis of disturbances and compensations, and of the process according to which affirmations and negations internalize themselves (behaviors of type α and γ of §13) and lead to internal variations of operational and reversible systems.

On the whole, however complex the different aspects of this development—perhaps because of their very complexity they are the source of ever new advances—the general traits which appear to characterize them can be attributed to a relatively few interactions for which "increasing equilibration" forms the expression. But the description of this development depends on a double condition: not reducing it either to a progression toward static equilibrium, or to a pure evolutionism which would suggest a radical becoming and forget the various vectors. However, any improvement is orientated in the direction of a more advanced coherence directed by internal necessity.

Appendices

Appendix A

REPLY TO A
FEW OBJECTIONS

The successive versions of this essay have given rise to criticisms by devoted colleagues to whom I am most grateful. I am particularly indebted to C. Nowinski. Naturally I took these questions into consideration, but incriminated propositions may still exist, and it might be useful to review them here.

1. The first criticism is that, if all disturbances release a regulation and if all regulations include a compensation orientated toward the equilibrium, the proposition is always true and consequently tautological. The reply was partly furnished in §4 and 5. Generally speaking, a disturbance is merely an obstacle holding an assimilation in check (whether it derived from a fact contradicting a judgment or from a situation which prevents achieving a goal). It can, therefore, release a regulation, but there can also be more or less durable incomprehension of the situation, rejection of the scheme, action blocking, etc., and consequent reaction which reveals an absence of regulations. Moreover, if there is a regulation, it cannot compensate, as is the case when a

positive feedback reinforces an error. To the arguments already furnished, let us now add that the possible reactions to the external or internal disturbance are not to be classified into complete or useless responses, but that multiple intermediaries exist between total success and failure indicated by more or less crude, or advanced, tests of the compensating regulations. Now, this observation is important to note, for just like the equilibrations which are crowned with success, it raises the general problem of explaining this success and the reason for such interactions as well as the reasons for the more complete processes which concern us.

2. The second criticism is that, if it is legitimate to refer to various types of regulations (and attempt not to confuse them), how can we give to the notion of compensation an indefinitely enlarged significance, when to achieve precision we should limit it to the process of negative feedback? At the end of this essay, we will submit a synthetic reply to such an objection which will doubtless return quite often.

It certainly is necessary to analyze in detail the elementary varieties of regulations, but we lack sufficient facts concerning behavior and must return to this question. On the other hand, it appears certain—and this suffices for us—that any regulation includes processes operating in opposite directions, for example, the two directions implicit in any feedback, and variations in "more or less." In both these cases we find an adjustment of positive and negative characteristics. Certainly we can maintain that "plus-plus" relations in positive feedback correspond to "plus-less" and "less-plus" relations in negative feedback. As already stated, we find the correction of a deficit, the filling of a gap, etc., without which positive feedback would be useless, or we see that the two "pluses" are orientated in opposite directions, as in a situation where "more resistance" leads to greater effort.[1]

---

[1] In model IA of Chapter Two, a plus-plus relation intervenes in the transmission of the movement from the agent to the subject. How-

This general characteristic of regulations—for lack of which we would be unable to see how the actions could be improved by their adjustment—makes it possible to give compensations a synthetic and formal definition: there is compensation when, in reply to a disturbance, a subject attempts to coordinate a situation's positive and negative characteristics; the compensation is complete when the implied negations correspond to all the affirmations. This definition has the double advantage of being applicable to the final (logico-mathematical) operational systems, which are entirely compensating, and of foreseeing degrees in the compensations, ranging from their absence as indicated by unfruitful tests (recalled under section 1) to the more or less developed forms which function with their highly diverse contents. With this definition, the diversity of the contents no longer constitutes a defect, since we find in each the same problem, so difficult for young subjects to handle: the need to coordinate the positive and negative aspects of the situations, which constantly requires going beyond observables.

3. We now understand the reason for the laws of evolution which we were able to free. First, the reason for the initial nonbalance, resulting in the necessity for compensations, is the systematic primacy of the positive characteristic of observables and the assimilation at the beginning of affirmations almost exclusively, without negations. The first negations are imposed from without, in the form of exogenous disturbances, and the subject's first behaviors consist in countering them by suppressions or accommodations; hence we see type a behaviors as described in §13. Next the disturbances and the compensations are gradually internalized and integrated into the system (behavior types

---

ever, in this case, there is no regulation, because the transmission is allowed as a function of simply covariations and of a direct causal inference. Nevertheless, an operational compensation intervenes between what the agent spends and what the subject gains (transmission, with conservation, of mv and of $\frac{1}{2}mv^2$).

β and γ). But what is the method for this internalization which we have been accused of not defining sufficiently?

First, the functional reason for the internalization is simple: the initial compensations are always incomplete because of the considerable spread between the affirmations and the negations and because of the necessity initially to construct them by means of inferential and logical coordinations (elaboration of classifications, systems of relations, etc.). In other words, the regulations are insufficient, and the additional compensations which they require then produce the regulations of regulations whose existence constitutes ipso facto an internalization.

On the level of functional reasons for internalization (and without again recalling the necessary formation of regulators which furnish structure) we do not leave the field of compensations, since the refinement of regulations is inseparable from the progress of compensations. We could say here that the compensations constitute a necessary but insufficient condition for the equilibration, since the essential driving force for the equilibration comes from the perfecting of regulations which yields a progressive self-organization. But this means dissociating—in the form of separate conditions—the construction factors and those of compensation, and they are inseparable, since construction results from regulations of regulations (from the second to the nth power) and thus requires a continual improvement of the compensations.

4. The chief objection we encounter is that we confine ourselves to description without presenting an explanation. In replying to this, let us begin by stating the criterion which distinguishes between the two approaches. Description ascertains a certain number of general facts (stages of a development, directions followed, relations between one characteristic and another, a formation's strength, etc.) but without exceeding the level of verifications (observables), or determining the degree of generality of the facts. Explanation begins the moment we can see the reasons for these general facts, which means we relate them to one

another, or to others still unknown, by a link of deductive thought orientated toward a theoretical construction. It goes without saying that many levels of this thought can be distinguished both from the viewpoint of the internal logical inferences and from the experimental verification of a theory based on a science of facts. With the first of these two viewpoints, all intermediaries are possible between the connections, whose necessity remains likely, and the articulations of a properly formalized theory. With experimental deduction, we likewise find all the degrees of transitions between an overall agreement with the facts—whose diversity makes varied cross-checking possible—and a verification made point by point.

We can boast neither of an advanced deductive theory nor of an agreement between verified facts, except when cross-checking between the results of varied research has been possible. Nevertheless, we believe we have gone beyond the level of description on a certain number of issues where it becomes possible to refer to "reasons." Some of these refer to functions—that is, they limit themselves to indicating the necessity of an observed function—others are "structural," responding to a causal mechanism.

It is futile to discuss further the functional reasons. It is clear that if knowledge is due to assimilation and accommodation activities, it requires their being placed in equilibrium. Moreover, if a systematic symmetry of positive and negative characteristics exists at the initial stages, it goes without saying that this equilibration could not be immediate and still require a durable play of compensating regulations which deal at first only with the observables and the elementary coordinations. Each limited success—i.e., each is incomplete, but the beginning of a success—requires an improvement of these regulations. Contrary to the propositions which equate knowledge with a copy of reality or deploy innate structures, the notions of assimilation and of accommodation actually imply the necessity of a continuous functioning to ensure the supply of material for assimilation and submission to the accommodation. In distinction to organic assimilations and accommodations, which deal only with the substances and energies necessary for the conservation of structures, the cognitive assimilations and accommodations, while continuing these biological processes, cannot help but constantly increase their field (which, at the limit, would include all of reality plus the progressive world of possibilities). But this indefinite increase would not be considered a simple accumulation, since the nature of the assimilation ensures an effective integration—in other words, a play of relation leading to the formation of totalities recurrently enclosed on themselves.

Let us return to the structural reasons which we can reduce to the following seven:

(1). The first, which conditions all the rest, is derived naturally from the characteristic of interdependence (or the formation of cycle) of components of any assimilating system (elementary schemes and all others up to those of the superior ranks). When we speak of assimilation, hence integration, we necessarily refer to a previous system which is more or less bound up or durably integrated according to its level. If not durably integrated, the assimilation would be reduced to contingent "associations." This is the situation at the very outset of the first sensorimotor assimilations (with reflexive schemes whose integration is therefore hereditary), but it exists only until superior formal assimilations take place.

(2). The fundamental factor of a cognitive equilibrium is the conserving action exercised by all the systems (of any rank) on their parts once they are finished. It is true that this completion is variable. Therefore, a reinforced or weakened stability is achieved by new accommodations. But this completion remains essential to every stage, because it results from a previous functioning of an assimilation and the conservation of the whole cycle. The subordination of parts is the condition *sine qua non* for the continuation of this functioning. It is this conserving power of the whole which constitutes the regulator orientating the regulations every instant—and in the form of an imperative demand.

Either the insertion of new assimilations and accommodations is possible in the whole cycle, or there is a rupture of this cycle and abandonment of the system.

(3). The totalities thus elaborated never represent a final condition, since the regulation of their functioning produces not only modifications but sooner or later produces anticipations which then give birth to "reflectings" (§6). As a result, the actions or operations used as instruments in a previous structure can become thematic objects of thought on a new level (or of assimilation, depending on the level). Consequently there is an expansion of the structure, with extension of variations in "more or less" and in correspondences between the negations and the positive characteristics. The entire history of mathematics stems from such a process of "reflecting abstraction" explaining the formation of new structures based on the preceding, and we see this at the beginnings of psychogenesis.

(4). This "reflecting," revealed in the formation of new levels, is inseparable from a reorganizing "reflection," which involves ever more advanced compensation of negations and affirmations. Neither the reflecting nor this reflection is foreign to the process of regulations. If the reflecting results from an awareness of the adjustment in play (hence the thematizations of previous operations), the reflection constitutes a new regulation which grafts itself onto the preceding regulations. The formation of regulations of regulations is thus explained by an action of the reflecting abstraction as a differentiation of the same mechanism and not as a new factor introduced from without. The reflecting and the reflection constitute two aspects of the same reality and express, by the same result, what constitutes the formation of operations on operations. We see why the earlier structure is better understood or, more precisely, is really understood only when integrated into the following (this is again evident in mathematics as well as in psychogenesis).

(5). We then reach the paradoxical insight that each structure requires the following for the realization of the possibilities opened by the preceding. In fact, if the regulator of the preceding is driven by the power of the totality of its cycle, the conservation of the following depends from the beginning on the conservation of the former in its cyclic form, yet must expand it. This means that the new assimilations and accommodations constitute both the derivatives and the support of the preceding, since they enlighten them by completing them (this provides an example of any recurrent generalization).

(6). The increasing equilibration, defined as a better equilibrium and distinct from a merely earlier better-stabilized equilibrium, unifies the constructions and the compensations and is therefore not explained only by the need for a supply of assimilation schemes (theoretically unlimited but which alone would only lead to accumulation). It permits the forms of the previous structures to become (by reflexive thematization) the contents of superior forms which can then be completed by new contents thanks to a kind of logico-mathematical generalization which creates its own contents by the indefinite combination of direct and inverse operations (cf. the passage of natural numbers, N, to whole numbers, Z, to rationals, Q, and to real numbers, R). Here, the problem of the increasing equilibration can therefore be confused with that of the fecundity of mathematics. This is the level where the regulations of regulations finally lead to the state of operations on operations or of operations at the nth power. In other words, the regulations of regulations which, from a certain level on, consist of new "reflections" on the preceding, result in the continual construction of forms as yet unknown and including as contents structures from previous levels, while at the same time completing them by the creation of other contents produced by the operations inherent in these superior forms.

(7). It is clear that this internal construction is accompanied by external attributions of objects. There are therefore successive levels of causality and functional interactions of logico-mathematical and scientific thought.

Appendix B

MORPHISMS
AND REGULATIONS

The Center of Genetic Epistemology has recently been engaged in studying, at every level of mental development, the relations and morphisms established by the subject which are indispensable to the formation and to the organization of operations. Here then is another perspective which at first glance seems foreign to that of regulations and equilibration adopted in the present work. It is useful to point out, however, that at present the concepts referring to morphisms and regulations are constantly complementary, and that the one will never replace the other but, on the contrary, will summon it. There are two reasons for this.

The first is that all regulations imply correlations. We have in fact defined regulation (§4) by the effects exerted on the repetitions of an action by their previous history—by the corrections or reinforcements intervening in the repetition of an action which are determined by the results obtained during the preceding tests. This definition of regulation—whether the regulation is overall or detailed, imprecise or precise, still unfruitful or already successful—

implies comparisons, hence correlations, and of every kind; i.e., between the new results and older ones, between this or that aspect of a result, and between this or that part of an action, etc. The sole fact of applying a regulation several times to the same scheme or to the same situation (whether this scheme is modified on the way or at first remains unchanged) constitutes an "application" in the sense of the theory of relations. In short, cognitive regulations would not be possible without correlations of various forms, partial or more or less complete. The study of morphisms is therefore not only useful but even indispensable when we wish to analyze the technique of regulations. However, in this work we have ignored technique and limited ourselves to the interventions and the compensations which regulations can involve.

The second reason for the necessary union of the concepts of morphisms and regulations is that the evolution of morphisms during cognitive development gives rise to all kinds of corrections, complements, and reinforcements. This means that they also obey internal laws of equilibration and present their own increasing equilibrations.

In our outline we have, in fact, noticed the following stages. Generally, beginning merely with a search for "bijections," the subject, under the effect of the resistance of objects, later undergoes "surjective" and "injective" relations, but without their reciprocities (which we will call, respectively, "multijections" and "subjections"), because of the inability to find again one or more of the characteristics or elements surjected in totalities, and above all, because of the lack of understanding of the incomplete relations or subjections (hence in particular we see inclusion difficulties; see §30). When the reciprocities are grasped, the composition of applications and their reciprocities becomes possible. The formation of morphisms follows, if we characterize them not only by the progress of correspondences dealing with the relations but by the terms (in comprehension as in extension), expressly the transferable nature of these generalized correspondences (as distinct from their applications which only deal with a given situation). The compositions between morphisms then permit the formation of special "categories," and the morphisms between categories (known as "*foncteurs*") make it possible to achieve the general categories, which can then be expressed in operational structures by the introduction of reversibility by inversion and the quantifications they involve.

It is clear that such an evolution is based on an equilibration, not because the progress consists in completing an unfinished system, implying compensations by mere filling of gaps—which would be a tautological description—but because (as should be the case if we wish to speak of compensations) the difficulties the subject has to surmount are shown in the form of nonbalances caused by obstacles or resistances of new contents to the forms until now found to be sufficient. The victory over these obstacles opens new possibilities. This is what we try to show in detail from our observations.

Appendix C

PHENOCOPIES
AND INTERNALIZATION
OF DISTURBANCES

We have tried to show in §13 how a disturbance, at first felt as exterior, gives rise to a cancellation (type a behaviors), then creates an accommodation of the subject's schemes (type β behaviors), and is finally an internal variation within the system (type γ behaviors). This process can be regarded as having biological roots. In formulating origins in terms of *order from noise*, von Foerster showed how "noise" first having an effect only beyond the organism could become a source of useful information.

Above all, the succession of behaviors from type a to type γ constitutes—from the cognitive viewpoint—a passage from the exogenous (an empirically noted variation) to the endogenous (the same variation operationally reconstructed). Such a passage finds its correlate in the biological phenomenon currently known as "phenocopy." It is defined as a replacement of a phenotype, due to pressures on the surroundings, by a genotype caused by the organism's genic

activities which then reproduces endogenously the characteristics of the initial phenotype. Now, without referring to
heredity in the Lamarckian sense, or even using recently
revealed information about the ARN's actions on the ADN
in certain special cases, we have tried[1] to interpret phenocopies observed among the lymnaea and sedum in the following manner. If the surroundings produce only an ordinary phenotype, included in the previous "standard
reactions," there is no reason why it should give rise to an
endogenous reconstruction. On the other hand, if the
exogenous variety is the source of a more or less important
nonbalance, it can even sensitize the regulating genes corresponding to the organism's modified regions. In this
event, this sensitivity naturally does not yield information
about the characteristics of the newly produced exogenous
varieties nor about what is required in order to produce a
reaction. There is merely a nonbalance backlash created,
which indicates by feedback the existence of a disturbance
in the syntheses controlled by the genome. The latter "replies," according to the accepted expression, with the production of more or less uncertain variations and, like the
others, they are submitted to mechanisms for selection.
Now, in the special situation in which the phenotype dis-
turbs the equilibrium of the internal milieu, it is the equilibrium which will function as the instrument of selection.
Thus there is "organic selection" in the Baldwin sense, and
it is therefore to be expected that the endogenous variation
finally resembles the phenotype, since it was forced by se-
lections to mold itself in the form determined by the phenotype.

Usually the phenotypes are closely linked to behavior,
and in plants, to the variations known as reactionals. The
passage from exogenous to endogenous varieties thus seems
to constitute a very general process relevant to every field
of life, from the organism to the cognitive functions. It goes

---

[1] See *Adaptation vitale et psychologie de l'intelligence: phénocopie
et sélection organique*, Hermann, 1974.

without saying that in cognitive functions the endogenous
and deductive reconstruction of links, at first empirical,
does not go back as far as the genome, since the development
of knowledge is dependent on equilibration and not
on innate programming. However the regulations play a
fundamental role in organic life and are included within the
genome. Whyte has even proposed a regulation of mutations, which takes account of the fact that it intervenes in
the phenocopies, since it also depends on the internal milieu.

Generally speaking, any biological evolution, including
the cognitive functions, is at first dominated by the permanent necessities of an equilibrium between the organism and
the external milieu (or between the subject and the objects), and is then characterized by the increasing autonomy
of the organism (or of the subject) in its self-organization,
and therefore by an increasingly internalized equilibration.
In this respect, the replacement of exogenous processes by
endogenous methods, revealed by phenocopies as well as by
the entire development of cognition, plays a fundamental
role.

Index